The Intended

David Dabydeen was born in Guyana, South America. He was educated at Cambridge University and University College, London, and now teaches at the University of Warwick. He has published two collections of poetry: *Slave Song* (1984), which was awarded the Commonwealth Poetry Prize, and *Coolie Odyssey* (1988).

The Intended

DAVID DABYDEEN

Minerva

A Minerva Paperback
THE INTENDED

First published in Great Britain 1991
by Martin Secker & Warburg Limited
This Minerva edition published 1992
by Mandarin Paperbacks
an imprint of Reed Consumer Books Ltd
Michelin House, 81 Fulham Road, London SW3 6RB
and Auckland, Melbourne, Singapore and Toronto

Reprinted 1992, 1993

A CIP catalogue record for this title
is available from the British Library
ISBN 0 7493 9850 7

Printed and bound in Great Britain
by Cox & Wyman Ltd, Reading, Berks

*for Simon Dabydeen
and Liz Burchell*

I

SHAZ KNEW MORE about sex than any of us boys and it was his erudition which drew me to him. At an early age he was versed in mysterious acronyms and abbreviations like CP, DOM, SUB, 'O' and 'A' levels, DIY, AC/DC, etc. Compared to Nasim, Shaz was positively brilliant. It was Nasim who startled me one day as we were waiting for a No. 88 bus at Tooting Bec Station by declaring that babies were born through the anus. He was adamant on the point and scoffed at my dissent. Even I, a complete virgin, knew that babies were born up-front, though the precise mechanism was still extremely puzzling.

Shaz was our oracle on this and other matters of a similar nature. Although curiously respected by us for his treasury of natural knowledge, he was despised by his father – an accountant's clerk – who never tired of calling him a dunce. The problem was that they were a Pakistani family, and therefore the arts and culture were not deemed worthy of study at school or university. What mattered were the sciences, medicine, law and computing. Accordingly, Shaz's elder brother took mostly science subjects for 'O' and 'A' levels (the G.C.E. examinations that is) and went on to study engineering at Aston University. The elder sister also trained as a scientist and became a micro-biologist. Shaz's interest, however, was in the arts and for this he was heartily cursed by the entire family, including his mother, even though she could hardly read and write, add or subtract. The boy fancied poetic words and modern images. He amassed a collection of rock L.P.s and was fascinated by the surrealistic cover designs, splashes of electronically processed colours forming weird patterns and shapes: the contours of breasts and other half-glimpsed parts of the female body, futuristic animals in a dreamy landscape, huge boulders breaking and crashing into a river of molten ice, and his favourite of all – a huge black creature, half-man, half-bird, squatting over a nest of white eggs, enveloping them protectively in its broad wings, whilst from the edge of the frame the sinister barrel of a gun protruded. The back of the record sleeve contained poetic utterances, snatches of lyrics equally mysterious: 'I am an athlete of the Universe/Time lingers melancholy like a hearse', and so forth. He wanted badly to learn to play the guitar and compose his own music. His father called him a pansy.

I first met him at school during one lunch-break. He was in the company of his friend, Patel, taking no part in the adolescent skirmish of the playground. The white boys were howling and spinning around a football, or lashing out with cricket-bats, whilst Shaz and Patel stood against a wall watching. It was my first week at an English school and feeling isolated from the gang warfare I gladly sought out their company. Nasim, recently arrived from Pakistan, also gravitated in their direction and the four of us found ourselves together each schoolbreak. It was the regrouping of the Asian diaspora in a South London schoolground. Shaz, of Pakistani parents, was born in Britain, had never travelled to the sub-continent, could barely speak a word of Urdu and had never seen the interior of a mosque. Nasim was more authentically Muslim, a believer by upbringing, fluent in his ancestral language and devoted to family. Patel was of Hindu stock, could speak Gudjerati; his mother, who once visited the school to bring her other son, wore a sari and a dot on her forehead. I was an Indian West-Indian Guyanese, the most mixed-up of the lot. There we were together in our school blazers and ties and grey trousers, but the only real hint of our shared Asian-ness was the brownness of our skins. Even that was not uniform. Patel was Aryan, tall, fair-skinned, crisp and cared-for in appearance. He wore his clothes with a self-certainty, and I have always suspected that deep down he felt superior to the rest of us. Shaz was stoutly built, shabbily dressed and extremely black; Nasim, slim, was two shades darker than Patel and two shades less immaculate. I, the medium to dark brown West-Indian, was merely clumsy in my schoolclothes. The jacket seemed too heavy, it scratched my skin everywhere, the tie choked my neck, the

5

trousers flapped around my ankles and the shoes swallowed up my feet.

We were varied too in our different gifts. Patel was a slow learner in the classroom, always seeking to dodge the teacher's eye by sitting at the back and hiding behind the boy in front. He would blush and sweat and almost tremble when caught and asked to answer a question. His true talent, however, lay in pickpocketing, where the speed of his fingers appeared to contradict the sloth of his brain. He would practise his craft in the crowded school corridors, deftly lifting a handkerchief or packet of cigarettes from some boy's blazer and putting it into another's. He never took anything for himself, merely being content with the artistry of his performance. Moving from one lesson to another meant changing classrooms, and in the process Patel would be redistributing our possessions. It became an obsession with him and quickly earned him the nickname 'Pocket Patel' which served to identify him from the several other Patels in the school. There was 'Cricketer Patel', for example, whose cunning spin bowling matched his enigmatic, introspective character. He was intensely secretive, with no known friends, and outside of the school no one knew where he lived, no one ever met him in the streets. And 'Chemistry Patel', a quiet boy who was transformed into a showman in the lab when it came to mixing chemicals and balancing equations, and who went on to take a first at Cambridge. This Patel spoke English badly and therefore kept quiet on most issues to do with boyhood or school-life, preferring to smile broadly at anything said to him as if understanding

6

perfectly. What he lacked in the English language was overabundantly compensated for by his brilliant literacy in scientific formulae. 'Pocket Patel', though, was our favourite because he gladly instructed us in the art of theft. It was his only opportunity of leadership. Shaz took the role of victim, Patel the master, Nasim and I the pupils. Patel would move up to Shaz, talk to him, all the time feeling for his pocket, manoeuvring him into a position where his pocket became vulnerable. After this rehearsal we would be invited to perform, and he would patiently coach us as we fumbled about Shaz's body. However much we practised, though, we could not match Patel's dexterity, which secretly pleased him.

What also endeared Patel to us was his fund of knowledge about films. Stupid as he was in the class-room, he possessed an outstanding knowledge of Holly-wood and had seen material that was barred to us. He went to every film at the local cinema at least once, but especially the 'X'-rated ones, for he was tall enough to pass for eighteen and, more importantly, his cousin was a ticket-seller. The cinema was some ten minutes' walk from the school. I passed it every day, gazing at its poster displays of semi-naked flesh smeared with lipstick, wishing I were Patel. Through the glass doors I could see the auditorium with its hot-dog kiosk and ticket office, and beyond that two thick, padded doors, guarded by a uniformed usherette, behind which lay the amphitheatre of unspeakable pleasures. It would be a trial of strength, a test of masculinity, to overcome all the obstacles between the glass door and the padded doors; to walk through the brightly-lit auditorium, buy a ticket casually, avoiding the knowing eyes of the ticket-seller and, as you passed the kiosk, pretend not to see the smirk on the face of the attendant; as you carelessly handed your ticket to the young usherette, try desperately not to notice the loose button on her blouse that exposes a morsel of breast; she tears the ticket and the noise is enormous, like the rending of a veil, but you attempt a smile, seeming to hear nothing and waiting for an eternal moment for the half-ticket, all the time pressurised by the memory of her body, the scent of it. You push the door and with a sense of immense relief you find it actually opens, and you stumble nonchalantly over a bubble in the carpet towards the deliciousness of a dark amphitheatre; your first, automatic reaction to the darkness is to cough, as if to locate your body, to ensure that it came with you and was not left abandoned in the foyer. I began to admire the courage of Patel, his meeting with an unknown darkness.

Of the group it was only Nasim who harboured a secret dislike of Patel, a feeling I suspect that was grounded in ancient Muslim-Hindu hostilities. There was no end of bickering between them when war broke out in 1971 between India and Pakistan on the issue of Bangladesh. None of us understood the global reasons for the conflict but we were thrilled and appalled by newsreels of carnage in the jungle. The Irish were simultaneously blowing up the streets of Belfast on television, and there was probably a connection between the two theatres of war but we didn't know quite what. Primitive feelings of loyalty began to emerge from our ignorance, so that Patel suddenly rediscovered his Indianness in a mannish surge of pride, especially when Pakistan was on the retreat, and Nasim was glum for days, refusing to speak to any of us. Shaz did not take sides, being almost wholly Anglicised. He was into rock music, and when George Harrison organised a concert in aid of flood-afflicted Bangladesh Shaz bought the record. (The English children in the meantime had composed their own cruel lyric about Bangladesh, a variation of the tune of 'riding along on the crest of a wave' . . .) His father thumped him one day when he played it too loudly and confiscated his record-player. This was Shaz's only involvement in the sub-continental war. I favoured Patel; being once a Hindu, my mind had been indelibly stained by the old Guyanese Hindu proverb about 'never trusting a fulla-man'. In all my years of boyhood in Guyana I had never once been assaulted or betrayed by a Muslim, yet the old suspicion lurked mysteriously in my mind like a lust waiting to be revealed and gratified.

To nobody's surprise a fight broke out in the playground between Patel and Nasim. For weeks they had been squabbling, refusing to pass the ball to each other in our football skirmishes, or colliding deliberately in chasing after it. One lunch-time, Patel, in full pursuit of glory, swerving past one defender, then another, the goal-mouth yawning before him, was tripped up from behind by an awkward thrust of Nasim's foot. He fell headlong, hitting his face against the brick wall. The game stopped. We watched Patel crumpled against the wall as if dead. Nasim stood a few yards away, his hands plunged in his blazer pockets as if hiding them from sight. He could not bear to look at us, or at Patel. He hoped he was invisible but all eyes were focused on him accusingly. Patel suddenly uncoiled, leapt up and hit out blindly, cuffing a startled Nasim on his face. They both fell, jerking and tearing at each other. We surrounded them and after allowing a reasonable period for the play of passions (two or three of the more bloodthirsty among us were in fact eagerly spurring on the combatants) we coaxed them apart. From Nasim's point of view – not that he would have had any, for his eyes were badly swollen – it was a fortunate intervention. That same evening the television flashed news of the surrender of Pakistan. Patel had won the fight and the war.

From that moment it seemed that defeat was Nasim's fate. A series of calamities befell him, and he failed his English G.C.E. examinations that year when we all passed – even Patel.

Patel's uncle had written out for him two long descriptive passages: the first heralding dawn, the sun hanging like a fat gold watch in a pocket of cloud; the second, evening, the moon smearing the sky in a glaucous green. These passages were gorged with sweetmeats selected from *Roget's Thesaurus*: splendid adjectives like 'irridescent', 'pristine' and 'sepulchral'. All Patel had to do was to memorise the two passages. In opening his essay, whatever the topic set by the examiner, he would use the dawn description, and he would close in a burst of lyricism about dusk. For the middle of the essay he was abandoned to his own devices. His uncle warned him to pad out the middle with a simple story and not to hazard the use of dimly familiar polysyllabic words, of which Patel claimed, out of wounded pride, to know one or two. The rest of us shuffled nervously into the examination room, but Patel was swishing with confidence, his head singing with the poetry of nature. We opened our examination sheets with some fear, nausea welling up in our stomachs, one or two of us already on the brink of fainting. Patel didn't even bother to read his sheet, merely turning it over and looking at it to follow procedure and avoid suspicion. As soon as the invigilator bellowed 'Begin', Patel began to fill the page, pouring out his exquisite soul, its emotions recollected in the tranquillity of the examination room. He scribbled vigorously in case he had a lapse of memory between one sentence and another. It was only after he had exhausted the dawn chorus that he wiped his brow from the effort and turned to the examination sheet, hoping to find an essay title that would fit the opening paragraph. And there it was, a gift of a title, or so it seemed, since it was obviously about nature: 'Tiger! Tiger! burning bright/In the forests of the night'. He could hardly suppress a whoop of relief as he settled down to the challenge of an unknown middle passage which would end in familiar moonlight. It was after he had stumbled through two or three sentences and studied the question again for clues to inspiration that panic seized him. 'In the forests of the *night*' . . . Fuck! They wanted the tiger described in the night-time, whereas he had begun his essay in daylight. What was he going to do? He chewed his pen for a full minute, glancing around to see what Nasim and the rest of his friends were up to, until the solution burst upon him like the very dawn in his opening paragraph: he would switch the memorised passages, starting with the moon like an aged spinster and black witch radiating light like the filaments of her broomstick, and culminating with the sun burnishing the clouds as it rose from the horizon's edge. The tiger would be hunted by men bearing torches and riding an elephant because it had snatched an Indian village baby whilst the family were asleep. It would be caught and killed early the next morning, and the meat given to the Untouchables to keep them happy in their tasks of emptying the garbage and weeding the roadside since only they were cannibalistic enough (Patel seemed to remember his mother saying this) to eat man-eating animals. He put pen to paper once again, congratulating himself for his cleverness in manoeuvring out of a tight spot ('unlike that bloody stupid tiger', he thought), imagining the surprised look on his uncle's face when he told him of the predicament and ingenious solution.

The shame of failing his examination further alien-ated Nasim, especially since he had always considered himself brighter than Patel. He became more and more aloof, and the group of four eventually dwindled to three. Then one day he failed to attend school. No one thought much of it. It was only as the days passed that we began to query his absence. A full week had gone by before Patel brought the news to us in the playground. His mother had met Nasim's mother in Tooting market and sobbed out the story. Nasim was in hospital. One night, returning home with his elder brother from the wedding ceremony of some relative, he had been set upon by five white youths lounging about at the mouth of the underground station, waiting for some action, something to brighten their lives. The youths caught sight of the brothers as they emerged and, emboldened by strength in numbers, taunted them, pushed them about. One or two moved in for the kill, flinging heavy punches when they sensed panic and helpless terror. Nasim, small-boned and agile, managed to dodge the worst, slip through the ring and sprint away. Four of the youths chased after him but they were fat and clumsy and he maintained a safe distance from them, his feet assuming a life of their own and taking him down unrecognisable back streets. He saw nothing, felt nothing but a nauseous lightness in his head and the automatic pounding of his feet on tarmac. As he ran his mind told him that he was striking a direction away from his home, for he didn't want to lead the youths there, where his mother was, and his young sister; his father was working nightshift, so the home was vulnerable, with large glass windows and a gate that could easily be kicked down, and the number of the house emblazoned on the outside wall for all to see (a dreadful mistake, he recognised now, which must be put right as soon as all this was over) which meant that they could keep coming back to the house, night after night, Paki-bashing packs of them, and his mother who could not speak English, and didn't know how to call up the police if the brothers were not there, and the father always at work, and other Asians in the street too frightened to come out and shout at the youths and scatter them, and the white neighbours who were nice and always said good-morning, nice-weather-we're-having, how-are-you, have-you-heard-the-latest-cricket-score, but who also had their own children to protect and big windows too, much bigger than theirs. There was a traffic light, it looked like Bedford Hill, he ran across the street, his eyes saw people on the other side, a car screamed about his ears, something slammed against his side.

We visited him on his twelfth day in hospital. His head was wrapped in bandages. The driver had only just braked in time, otherwise Nasim would have been dead. Patel tried to make a joke about how he looked like a Sikh warrior with a turban on. He looked small and lost, like pictures of hungry Third-World children we saw on television. I hated him. A strange desire to hurt him, to kick him, overcame me. Shaz brought him a music magazine and a home-made cake decorated with bright red cherries which his mother had baked specially. I watched him, not knowing what to say, distressed, feeling a bitter contempt, especially at the sight of his stupid, helpless eyes peeping out between the bandages. He was a little, brown-skinned, beaten animal. His wounds were meant for all of us, he had suffered them for all of us, but he had no right to. It was Nasim's impotence which was so maddening, the shamefulness of it. I knew immediately that Patel, Shaz and I could never be his friend again, because he had allowed himself to be humiliated. We would avoid him in school because he reminded us of our own weakness, our own fear.

Patel swore with the fervour of renewed brotherhood that he'd catch and tear them apart. The three of us would set upon them once we found out who they were. Shaz and I nodded faintly. Nasim said nothing, just blinked stupidly. Perhaps he couldn't speak anyway. Maybe his jaw was cracked. We left him to his family, several of whom had turned up from as far away as Sheffield. His brother, who had managed to escape with a few minor bruises, hung around us disconsolately, the red stripes on his face like badges of shame. I fancied he looked like Patel's tiger vanquished by the hunt. I was glad to escape the peculiar hospital smell of starch and bleach and medication. In any case, the mother was beginning to rub Nasim's hand and weep, quietly, so as not to disturb the neighbouring patients and their visitors. I was embarrassed for all of us, for the several Asians wrapped in alien, colourful clothes who whispered to each other in a strange tongue and crowded protectively but belatedly around their beaten son. No doubt they presented a right sight to the white patients and guests who kept eyeing them. I was sure I could hear a few giggles. I knew then that I was not an Asian but that these people were yet my kin and my embarrassment. I wished I were invisible.

It was the same feeling of shame that all of us, whether Indo-West-Indians or real Indians, felt at the sight of our own people. Nasim and I who both lived in Balham would often travel home together after school. Whenever an Asian sat next to us on the Tube, dressed in a turban or sari, we would squirm with embarrassment, frozen in silence until the doors opened to release us at our destination. The peculiar environment of the Tube intensified our self-consciousness, especially as there was no view out of the window to distract our attention. The white English remained utterly silent for the whole journey, hiding behind a newspaper or concentrating on a point in space as if in profound contemplation of the mysteries of nothingness, or else reading and re-reading the advertisements selling pregnancy predictors, fresh-breath capsules, bargain holidays in Spain. Asians were invariably curious about each other, and furtive glances would be exchanged, eyes meeting and withdrawing in an instant as we assessed one another to find out how long since the one sitting opposite arrived in the society, and from which part of the sub-continent, and how he was getting along with the new life. We could not talk to each other openly in the way people in Asia or the Caribbean offered greetings or waved hands, even to utter strangers, as a form of recognition that we were all human beings, and that today the sun was beating down on the one world, a street of which, somewhere in Jamaica, Guyana, India, we happened to be walking down when we met and ceased being strangers for a moment. In the London Underground we were forced into an inarticulacy that delved beneath the stone ground and barrier of language, whether Urdu, Hindi or Creole, and made for a new mode of communication: as the train trundled through a dark tunnel we flashed glances at one another, each a blinding recognition of our Asian-ness, each welding us in one communal identity. In the swift journey between

Tooting Bec and Balham, we re-lived the passages from India to Britain, or India to the Caribbean to Britain, the long journeys of a previous century across unknown seas towards the shame of plantation labour; or the excitement with which we boarded *Air India* which died in a mixture of jet-lag, bewilderment and waiting in long queues in the immigration lounge at Heathrow – just like back home, the memory of beggars lining up outside a missionary church for a dollop of food from a white hand, and women with cracked lips crowded at a standpipe shoving enamel bowls to catch the few slow drops. In the glitter of duty-free shops and fluorescent lights you cannot hide the memory of poverty. The thick, unfamiliar feel of carpet in which your waiting feet seem to sink further unsteadies your balance, feet already strapped in unaccustomed shoes and for twelve hours, the time since you first put them on as you departed for the airport, lost from sight or contact with bare earth. The white man behind the desk is asking many questions. He is inspecting everything, sending some people to a room behind him where they are to be interrogated further. People are opening handbags, giving him extra pieces of paper. He reads. He is still not satisfied. They open up more handbags and feed him more paper.

Nasim and I got out, leaving the Asian behind. We were relieved to be on the platform, lost, invisible in a movement of people towards the escalator. He was more deeply afflicted with a sense of shame than I was. For me, it was partly an adventure into the past, a shame relieved by a vague wondering as I sat next to the Asian whether I too would have been wearing a turban if the British had not taken us away to the Caribbean. I had no knowledge whatsoever of India, no inkling of which part my ancestors came from, nor when they left, nor even their names. My only contacts with India were the days spent at my grandmother's house in the countryside of Guyana. We grew up in the town, New Amsterdam, and during the school holidays I would be put aboard a bus bound for Albion village with a bag stuffed with clothing, and a mango to eat on the journey. My mother always put me on the 'Duke of Kent' because the driver, Kumar I think his name was, was a friend of the family and did not charge me a fare. It was a better bus than the 'Royal Princess', 'Westminster', 'Ghengis Khan' and the other vehicles plying the Berbice route because it had a reputation for speed. Kumar loved nothing more than mashing down the makeshift road between New Amsterdam and Albion, the great rubber tyres churning up clouds of red dust that mixed with diesel fumes and plumed behind us. It descended upon and roared past the Berbice villages, blazing its horn, leaving behind a wake of red and black dust, like a memory of its rage, that slowly spread against the sky, but could barely stain it, the blueness from one end of the earth to the other absorbing and neutralising all. The villagers, startled for a moment, settled down to the calm of the sky.

I sat squashed against a window, sharing my seat with two fat women bearing baskets of vegetables on their laps. Although the bus was packed, Kumar would still stop to pick up passengers along the way, fired by a blend of compassion and commercial good sense. They were country people, accustomed to lingering by the roadside for long periods under a fierce sun for the bus's approach. The toot of Kumar's horn carried for miles, signalling impending relief from the tedium and sun scorch. They gathered their belongings together and the coins for the fare, waiting to catch sight of the bus. Somehow they managed to squeeze in, finding space even for their market goods, which consisted of everything from live chickens with their legs tied together to bunches of ripe bananas which suffused the bus with a sweet smell, blending oddly with the aroma of engine oil and human sweat. It was a long, spectacular ride past villages of wooden or mud houses, many sporting Hindu flags of reds and whites in their yards; children playing cricket pausing as we passed and waving the coconut branches they used for bats, or diving into water under the watchful eye of their mothers beating clothes on the canal bank; old men, the receptacles of charity, propped on sticks, mincing along the road, bearing sacks on their backs; young men gathered in the forecourts of rum shops slapping down dominoes; people of all ages ankle-deep in ricefield mud, plucking at plants with frantic energy. The drabness of shacks which comprised many villages was occasionally disturbed by temples and mosques, their whitewashed domes and elegant turrets imparting an incongruous splendour to the landscape. These places of worship were the treasures of the community, exhibitions of the beauty and idealism of their barefoot lives.

19

We reached the top of the escalator, climbed some stairs, emerged into light again and made our way home.

When he was released from hospital Nasim stayed at home for a while and I would go to see him. I missed him at school, even though our friendship could never be the same. We lived not far from each other, and travelling home together we would strike up long conversations about anything that came into our heads, especially when we decided to walk instead of taking the bus or Tube, saving the fares for a packet of cigarettes. It would take us nearly an hour to wend our way from Tooting to Balham, and we would light up as soon as we were a safe distance from the school. I cannot now remember the substance of our conversations, except that they invariably focused on sex and religion. Nasim had an irritating habit of discussing the two topics simultaneously, refusing to separate fleshly desire from respect for Allah. All of us growing up in London were swamped with images of sex which had no bearing on morality, or indeed any kind of value at all, apart from the commercial. Such images were self-contained, thrilling in themselves. The billboards we passed on our way carried provocative photographs of fleshy lips sucking at a cigarette, or teenage girls in black tights sprawled on the bonnet of the latest motor car. Nasim was impervious to such loose images, adamantly asserting an Islamic connection between things and the spirit, arguing that Mohammed penetrated every crevice, irradiated every blind desire. I preferred the girls sprawling and free, than to see them bundled in black cloth, with Mohammed, fierce, dark, masculine, hairy-chested, oriental, towering over them with his camel. 'Life should be fun,' I argued, but he called me a pervert, comparing me to the men who toured the Bedford Hill area at night in the hunt for prostitutes. Allah was great, Mohammed was his prophet, and I was a West-Indian who had strayed from these truths, he said, sucking at the cigarette and coughing, because he had not yet acquired the skill of drawing in the smoke fully so that it suffused the lungs with warmth, then blowing it out in contentment. After smoking we would suck sweets vigorously until we reached Balham, to erase the evidence of misdemeanour. 'You want to kill life,' I retaliated through the hole in a mint, evoking as illustration a fantasy of women tied up by religious cords and being flagellated for their sins. He was appalled at my disgraceful travesty of Islamic tenets, chewing loudly and accusing me of misconstruction and irreverence, which he put down to my having lived too long in England where people cared nothing for family, dumping their parents in old people's homes, marrying and breeding and divorcing and bequeathing the children to the welfare, abusing their own kids or abducting other peoples'; where every Sunday saw the churches empty and the pubs packed with dart-throwing louts relaxing from the hooliganism of the football match the day before, building up their strength for next Saturday's warfare. Sometimes he would be so startled and carried away by the force of his own invective that the cigarette would become a weapon waving wildly in his hand, its burning tip both a beacon in the darkness and a bonfire to consume heathens at the stake. In the flow of ideas he would forget to puff, the light would eat down to the butt and burn his finger, so that he would drop it with a cry. In truth, these conversations were our childish ways of feeding our own smouldering desires. The positions we took in any argument did not matter; we both knew it was a game of words which allowed us to fantasise about sin and chastity. For this reason we always parted good friends, irrespective of the heat of the argument, and looked forward to the next bout of sweet-toothed aggression.

I walked up Bedford Hill on my way to visit Nasim, weaving my way through the market traders busily packing up their stalls after a long day's touting and bawling. Vans and makeshift carts littered the Hill, stuffed with unsold cheap clothing, plastic goods, fruit and vegetables. Canals of filthy water trickled along the edge of the pavement and emptied into the gutter, the grills half-blocked by refuse and rotting vegetation. The prostitutes were already gathering in twos and threes, waiting for the Hill to empty and darkness to fall before coming out in full numbers. They stood in the doorways of shops, shifting from foot to foot, or stamping as if to shake off imaginary snow. They smoked cigarettes and talked among themselves, interrupting their chatter to lean forward and smile whenever a motorcar passed. Even with a school blazer, jumper, vest, shirt and tie,

I could still feel the winter's chill close to my skin but they were dressed flimsily in half-coats and skirts barely covering their thighs. As I hurried past, eyes lowered in shyness, I smelled strong perfume, a burning scent, like flesh on fire I imagined, but also, curiously, like one of the smells from Nasim's hospital ward.

Rashida, his elder sister by a year, opened the door and led me to the sitting room. I waited nervously on the sofa whilst she fetched some tea. She wore a white shawl on her head, an Asian blouse and trousers. Nasim had gone out with his mother to visit relatives but would be back soon, she said, shyly, in one breath, as if unaccustomed to speaking to strangers. The room, decorated in green, with a reproduction painting of worshippers in Mecca hung over the gas fireplace, smelt sweetly of spices. I took the mug from her small, clean hand and put it to my mouth, sipping blindly. She sat opposite, as if to keep me company, out of politeness. I could not think of anything to say, and looked sheepishly about the room to avoid her gaze, hoping to find interest in other wise everyday objects like the plasterwork on the ceiling or the cluster of ordinary coloured ornaments on the mantelpiece: a lady holding an umbrella, a dog, a bird perched on a twig about to fly off (though it couldn't really go anywhere, being immobilised in plaster, and in any case one of its wings was badly chipped), and a pair of donkeys, the sight of which made me squirm and look away. On a small shelf at the far end of the room sat two dolls which caught my attention momentarily because they were dark-skinned, with thick curly black hair. I would have liked to have examined them more closely since I had never seen Indian dolls before, but I was swiftly overcome by a sense of shame. I turned instead to a tourist cloth-map of Pakistan, admiring the sequins around its border, noting its embroidered image of a mosque and of the unpronounceable names of cities, tracing the curves of the curious Islamic lettering. After a while she asked me whether I wanted a biscuit, and I heard myself saying no, much to my irritation since it would have been an immense relief to have had her leave the room. She settled back, found a magazine, and flipped through it. She must have uttered something else to me and a voice within me must have given (hopefully) some appropriate reply for I saw her get up, straighten her trousers and move out of the corner of my eye. I glanced up to see her leaving through the door, sensing only the sheen of her long black hair flowing from under her shawl.

I finally heard a voice outside, a rattling of the door, and Nasim and his mother came in. She greeted me with a startling warmth, putting her arms around me and kissing my cheek, almost as if I was one of her own sons whom she had not seen for some time. I felt foolish, instinctively withdrawing from her embrace.

'So nice you come see Nasim,' she uttered in broken English, 'you Nasim good friend, Nasim lucky,' and shouted something in Urdu. Nasim looked at me shyly, uncertain as to why he should be so fortunate to have me as a friend, and no doubt embarrassed by his mother's show of love. She called out again in Urdu at the top of her voice and I could hear Rashida coming down the staircase.

'You no drink tea and eat?' she asked me, and when Rashida came in she directed the question to her as if scolding the daughter for neglecting me. Rashida replied in Urdu, Nasim snapped at her in the same tongue and she turned and headed for the kitchen.

'I drink, but no hungry,' I offered, speaking slowly, dredging up the all-but-forgotten facility for Creole talk I had almost lost through lack of practice in the four years' residency in England.

'No, no, you come see Nasim, you eat,' she replied, taking off her coat to reveal a blue sequinned sari that immediately imparted light and colour to the drab room. In the protected environment of the home, the doors and curtains closed to alien eyes, her sari revealed a grace and dignity which suddenly banished all my boyish feelings of shame. She busied herself around the room, putting away a few loose books, balls of wool, re-arranging the cushions on the sofa, all the time calling out to Rashida.

'You bright boy, you eat,' she said, taking the plate of Indian sweets that Rashida had brought in and handing it to me before turning back to her task of tidying up the room.

'Nasim go Sheffield soon. Good for him, no? Balham too – too nasty place.'

I looked at him and felt sorry. He was being sent north to live with the rest of the family. It was safer there, the Asian community in Sheffield being more concentrated in particular areas, and so able to walk certain streets freely. At his new school no one need know that skinheads had beaten him up. He could recover his nerve and start life again.

'Nasim say how bright boy you, pass all exam.' She paused from her labours to gaze down at me with motherly pity in her eyes. I sat and nibbled stupidly at a white cream ball, the three of them standing like protective guards over me to make sure I would not go hungry. I suddenly felt treasured in their presence, strangely moved by a sense of family. I was small and shabby but they made me feel valuable, all because of some quality of mind they thought I possessed. In one of our conversations Nasim had confessed how much his parents admired me, and how they used to measure him against my school achievements, cursing him for not being as bright as I was, switching off the television and sending him upstairs to read a book. He was the instrument of his own discomfort, though, and often boasted to his parents how accomplished I was in all school subjects, no doubt in the hope of reassuring them that he kept the best company at school. Now, as his mother lavished love on me he knew that such an act contained implicit criticism of his failures. As I left she pressed some coins in my hand telling me to buy some milk for myself and making me promise to visit again.

'Nasim say your father give you to Welfare people to look after, your father drink very much whisky. Why your father leave your mother and run away to England and then send for you but not look after you?'

I didn't know what to say, and lingered at the doorway.

'How many years old you now?' she asked, breaking the uncomfortable silence.

'Fifteen,' I answered uncertainly, my mind doing a rapid calculation, 'it must be fifteen.'

'You not so old,' she doubted, gazing on my small body and feeling the bones of my arm, 'you look more eleven or twelve.'

I stood before her asserting my age, but in truth not knowing where the years had gone or how they had led up to this moment. Everything in my past seemed so jumbled up, all the people I knew as a child in another country were fading to a set of foreign-sounding names. They were like the characters in my geography textbook, vividly illustrated but unreal all the same. The intense colours in which the artist represented them only made them more unbelievable. I would have preferred to have seen them in plain photographs. It was more difficult to lie in photographs, people could be themselves more naturally.

'Why your father so wicked?' she resumed, letting go of my arm.

There was real anger in her voice, but seeing that I merely stared at my shoes glumly, unable to answer, her tone softened with pity.

'No matter, study hard, drink much milk,' she advised, and let me out of her house.

I walked down Bedford Hill feeling sorry for myself, wishing I had a family to go home to. Nasim's mother was like my grandmother who waited by the roadside and when I stepped off the bus at Albion village would take my hand tightly in hers and lead me across the dam to a drum of water in the yard. She took my bag upstairs and returned with a cotton vest, a powder tin and a towel. Then she unbuttoned my shirt and trousers, folded them neatly to one side, and poured water over me, rubbing in soap and washing it away, all the time interrogating me about how my mother doing, how my sisters, if the house roof repair yet, how my father treating all of we, if he does still drink rum and beat, if my mother is saving up she money. I spluttered out answers as best I could, the soapy water flowing down my face, making me squeeze my eyes or spit whenever I answered a question and the water ran into my mouth. She dried me vigorously, raised my arms and splashed powder everywhere. Then I was led fresh and naked to clean clothes and a plate of crab curry which I devoured, going back to the kitchen for more and licking the plate dry. I had the house all to myself, my three uncles having migrated to the city so as to get schooling. I dumped the plate in a basin of water and went downstairs, wandered about the yard, inspected the fowl in the pen my grandfather built, walked to the dam to throw a few stones in the trench and watch the circles rippling outwards, wandered back into the yard, lay in the hammock slung between two cherry trees and fell asleep.

I was awakened by the noise and smell of cows. It was late afternoon. My grandfather came through the gate, driving before him the small herd he had been tending in the savannah all day. After securing them in the pen he went to the tub of water to wash the mud from his body, muttering to himself all the while. I raised my head from the hammock to peep at him. He laid down his stick, took off his cloth cap, shook the dust from it and not having anywhere at hand to hang it, put it back on his head. He took a calabash shell, dipped it into the tub and drank from it, gargling and spitting out the water. Two loose hens scooted after it, thinking it a shower of corn. When they reached the spot and found nothing they lingered there foolishly. He fished out a rag from his back pocket, wet it, wiped his face and arms and slung it on the lip of the tub to dry. The rest of the water he scooped out and poured over his feet, rubbing one foot with the other vigorously until all the mud had dissolved. The hens, attracted by his agitation, walked towards him, pecking submissively at the ground around his feet. He shooed them away and when they ran in my direction he noticed me in the hammock.

'Eh! Eh! you come boy,' he called out, 'you hungry? Ma feed you?'

He took up his stick, went to the jamoon tree at the edge of the cow pen, prodded among the branches, snapped off a twig laden with purple fruit, and gave it to me. He reached into one of his deep pockets and dug out a golden-apple, a few loose guenips and some dounze. It made him happy to think he specially remembered that I was arriving today, and in driving the cows to the savannah, had stopped at various trees on the way, his long stick disturbing ants' nests, wasps, sleeping iguanas, and the odd tree-snake, to pick fruit for me. 'Cherry full on tree, you want cherry?' he asked, shaking one of the trees strongly so that the ripest and heaviest fell about my head. This is how I remember him, but perhaps in the treeless cold of Bedford Hill, vegetation rotting in the gutter and the whores climbing in and out of motorcars, I fabricate his memory, and his stick becomes a wand which with one wave conjures up a dream world of jamoon tree and tropical fruit whose tastes are now, like a magician's trick, still fresh in my mouth. Perhaps I am still dreaming in the hammock and the last day I saw him, when my mother sent me to Albion for the last time before taking me to the airport and the plane for England, never existed except as a romance of the mind. I knew it would be the last day I would see him. The morning before, very early, the air still dark and alive with the singing of crickets, he shook me awake. I was lying warmly in the bosom of my grandmother, her arm hugging me steadfastly. For some reason I never understood he slept in a separate room. He eased me from her grasp, plucked me up and took me to the posy at the far end of the room to urinate. Then he gave me some clothes to wear, took me to the kitchen, and after I had washed my face, I sat down at the table to eat a piece of bread and drink from an enamel mug steaming with hot milk. We headed for the savannah, walking forever that morning in semi-darkness, without exchanging a word. He strode ahead, deep in contemplation, whilst I trotted after him, fearful of losing sight of him and being left prey to the spirits of the bush. He would pause occasionally for me to catch up, knowing always, without having to look back, exactly how far away I was, and in what direction. The land breathed mist which sucked him in so that he disappeared momentarily, only to emerge shrouded in the half-light. I listened out for his stick scraping the earth and followed the sound. The ground was hard and painful to walk over, especially in places where cattle had trampled in mud which had dried out to leave small holes. My naked soles pressed against the sharp rims of these endless holes or else my foot would be caught or bruised in one of them, so that either I stumbled or else I somehow had to tiptoe across the terrain. My grandfather pressed on at a relentless pace, gliding over the land, his feet hardened by a lifetime of such journeys and instinctively knowing how to avoid the holes, how to find the firm flat spaces in between. The clearing came to an end and still he persisted, taking me through dense bush humming with mosquitoes. Invisible branches reached out to scratch my skin, birds screamed and flapped away wildly, a cobweb wrapped around my face. I scooted after him, careless of bruises, wanting him to stop but too terrified to cry out. My whole body was soaked with dew and sweat. At long last we stopped at the edge of a pond, and lifting me on his shoulders he waded across. We turned sharply to the left on the other side, picking up an abandoned path until we came to a circular clump of bush. There was no obvious entry, the path ending before this wall of undergrowth. He moved a little to one side, felt with his stick, and stepped in magically, his body seeming to dissolve into the bush. I heard him calling on the other side and followed his voice but could not find the opening. I stood there abandoned, but not caring any more what happened to me, just wanting to lie down and sleep and out of spite never wake up. My grandmother would come looking for me and find me, if she were lucky, and take me home. He must have sensed my despair for he emerged like a spirit from the bush, hoisted me on to his shoulders and took me in. On the other side of the wall was a clearing littered with huge rocks and there, tied to one of them, was a lamb. It had a long rope, and had explored the circle of the wall, trying to chew its way out. The broken twigs and leaves littering the circumference showed where it had explored the possibilities of escape. It ran up to us as if recognising its mother, raising a feeble bleat. It must have been trapped there for days, calling out plaintively, for its legs were shaky and its voice exhausted. My grandfather patted it on its head, untied the rope from the stone and led it to the wall. We eased our way out and retraced our steps to the pond, where I was again put on his shoulders whilst the lamb was led through the water, reaching the other end only by a miracle of effort. It was so exhausted that it had to be dragged home, my grandfather either pulling it violently by the rope around its neck or prodding it with his stick. I sat on his shoulders, too relieved by my own good fortune in being carried to care for the lamb's distress.

I know now why he was so strangely furtive on our return journey, stopping at the slightest unrecognised sound and waiting for a long time before moving on. He had stolen the animal, and hidden it away in the bush for a few days until the clamour of its owner had died down. Sheep-stealing was one of the greatest crimes in the village, and one habitually practised. Every villager stole his neighbour's sheep in preference to his own, not out of greed but out of habit. No one won or lost in these exchanges; in the end the number of sheep stolen and re-stolen balanced out and no one was cheated. Nevertheless there was a ritual of grief and outrage to be exhibited, the accusations flowed and were countered, the owner swore acts of vengeance outside the permitted boundaries of the law. After a few days the excitement died down and life resumed its even tone. Greater than the crime of sheep-stealing was that of being caught in the act. No man really worth his salt would be so foolish as to be discovered and to court the scorn of the village for years to come, indeed to the very end of his life. The tale of how so-and-so got caught would circulate in the rum shops for years, each teller infusing the narrative with his own gift of invention so that the event passed into the realms of legend, transmitted orally from one generation to the next. The poor thief and his family either succumbed to being the butt of ridicule or else they migrated to a distant village. It was because he was so jealous of his honour and reputation that my grandfather exercised such caution in hauling home the stolen lamb.

He killed it later that morning, under the jamoon tree, hidden from sight behind its trunk and the paling of the cow pen. I was lying in the hammock dreamily when I saw him come downstairs with a kitchen knife and a file. He walked to the cow pen and sharpened the blade. I followed him, sensing danger and excitement. The lamb was lying sideways in the mud, its fleece blotched with cow dung and its legs trussed up. It was breathing unevenly, and shuddered as if to get up when it sensed the approach of my grandfather from the corner of its eye. A few cows ambled over to satisfy a vague curiosity. He put one foot heavily on its body, pinning it to the ground. It kicked out impotently, the rope holding tight. He put the point of the knife to its throat, pushed it in and dragged it sideways. The animal froze, immobilised by the shock and rupture, then screamed and shook with such force that my grandfather's foot slipped from its body and he had to struggle to regain control. Blood showered from its neck but the lamb continued to whine and kick. Some more cows, attracted by the strange noise and agitation, wandered over and they stood chewing their cud and watching the killing with big unshockable eyes. The blood, gallons of it, flooded the spot, forming gutters, and trickling away in various directions. I felt a wet, warm flow about my feet, looked down to see my toes covered in blood. I tried to move away but could not until my grandfather barked at me to fetch a bucket of water.

He washed down the lamb and dragged it to the windowless room beneath the house which was used to store green bananas and other young fruit which needed ripening. 'Light lamp,' he ordered, and I raised the glass rim, scratched a match and the wick caught fire. I waited for more instructions, but he ignored me, taking up the huge knife and with skilful manipulation slicing open the carcass without spilling its contents, skinning the belly area of the lamb and pinning back the fleece so that when I held the lamp to it, the animal appeared to be wearing a coat on its back. It was hanging from the sling by its forelegs, the flesh of its neck and belly exposed. Through the thin layer of underskin I could see the bones and the coil of its intestines. My grandfather pierced the belly and the intestines slopped into a bucket on the floor. The room stank of raw flesh. I put down the lamp quietly and left. He called after me to fetch another knife but I went to the tub in the yard, drank some water and lay down in the hammock.

That night, groups of neighbours gathered in the yard drinking rum and eating curried lamb. They beat folk rhythms on old saucepans, empty bottles, calabash shells and danced and sang. One man entertained us by swilling kerosene in his mouth, holding a torch and blowing out a huge ball of flame.

'The boy going Englan,' my grandmother said proudly and tearfully, taking me from cluster to cluster to show me off. My grandfather drank so much that he crept away to a corner, folded his legs like a calf, hugged his rum bottle and started to cry. Whenever he was drunk he became sentimental and religious, muttering repentances for half-remembered misdeeds, or else bursting out in a spate of curses and resolutions of vengeance against the wickedness of his enemies. They laughed at him to begin with then ignored him, turning to their own food and drink. He eventually collapsed and had to be lifted upstairs and put to bed.

I woke the next day to the distant sound of cows bellowing in the savannah. My grandmother was making food in the kitchen, fussing among her pots, putting new wood in the fireplace. I sat down quietly, watching her move through the woodsmoke which, irradiated by sunlight, cast a glow around her whole body, so that all her movements glittered as in a dream. Fried plantains lay in a pan like strips of gold and the drops of oil spitting to the floor were diamond grains which she wiped up with an old cloth and shook out through the window. She wore a white Indian shawl over her head, tied behind in a knot like all the old women of the village, and around her ankle a thick twisted silver bracelet which her mother had bequeathed to her when she died, and which had come all the way from India. Once, as she lay down on the verandah bench, she called me to comb her hair, promising me a penny for each louse I killed. I killed none, getting my hands tangled up hopelessly in her long oily hair instead. She did not mind, lying there on the brink of sleep, her face brushed and cooled by the afternoon breeze. Desperate for pennies I clicked my fingernails, as if crushing a louse, loud enough for her to hear, and amassed in my mind a small fortune. 'Penny for grey hair,' she promised and I set about plucking out individual grey strands, which was a much easier exercise since there were many on her head to choose from. After a while, lulled by boredom and an excess of expected pennies, I looked for something else to do with her body and my eyes fastened on the silver bracelet. I eased her sleeping head from my lap and moved to the other end to

36

examine it. It was then that I noticed, instead of the silver bracelet, how cracked the soles of her feet were. There were lines everywhere, running in all directions, like a spider's web or a complicated map of the world tracing roads and rivers and other routes. She was born in Albion village, had never travelled out of the village, and would eventually die there, yet her feet mapped all the pathways of the world.

After I ate breakfast I went downstairs to wash. My grandfather gave me a blacksage twig with which to clean my teeth, showing me how to chew the ends so that they formed a brush. Although dead drunk the night before, he had woken up at first light to milk the cows and to do odd tasks about the house, cut some coconut branches to make palings for the fence, replace the rope around the cow-pen gate which a calf with toothache had chewed to bits, repair the odd holes in his fishing net. He was then ready to venture out into the village, laden with a basket of eggs and an old tin churn which contained carefully watered-down milk, one calabashful of well-water to one portion of milk. We went from house to house selling and bartering. He would rattle at the gate or call out names and people would come out with empty saucepans. He ladled out milk, handed over one or two eggs and collected the coins. Sometimes he would take a swig of rum instead of money, a length of rope, some nails, a chunk of homemade cheese or some fruit and vegetables. The basket slowly emptied of eggs and was piled up with a strange assortment of goods. Each house we went to presented a different spectacle. Some were brightly painted, with shining zinc roofs, others leaned feebly on their wooden stilts like beggars. Some had neatly trimmed yards, with a clean path leading to the front steps, and well-planted vegetable and flower gardens; others were thick with grass. Coloured flags fluttered on bamboo poles, distinguishing the Hindu houses from those of the Muslims and black people. He stopped outside Clarice's house and banged his churn. A voice answered hoarsely, and after a long wait an elderly fat black woman slowly descended the steps and made her way painfully towards us. One knee was wrapped in bandages soaked in spirits to ease the rheumatism. She wore a shawl over her head, just like my grandmother's.

'Eh! Eh! you bring de chile wid you,' she exclaimed on seeing me, 'and how is de Lord looking after you?' She stooped and kissed my head. Her daughter Jessica came up with a pot and my grandfather filled it with milk.

'Alright thanks Auntie Clarice, and I going Englan tomorrow-tomorrow,' I answered.

'Englan . . . Englan . . . so far and you never come back and see your Auntie Clarice,' she said with genuine sorrow in her voice.

I did not know what to say and looked away at my grandfather handing over the eggs.

'But you must tek education,' she recovered, 'you hear,' her voice becoming stern and cautionary, 'and pass plenty exam and work hard and get good job.' She instructed Jessica to go upstairs and bring something for me to eat.

'When de boy grow up in Englan he can turn Doctor

and come back and cure you foot, not so?' my grandfather asked.

I looked at Auntie Clarice's limbs, deformed with
pain, and nodded. She broke into a cackle of laughter.
'Only death can cure me, son, no medicine make by
man or witch. Only de Lord will succour me from
tribulation and tempest. I too damn old for me own
good.'

And truly she was old, her African face sprouting
hairs between the cracks, like a golden-apple seed. She
was as old as the village, old as the huge tamarind tree,
heavy with fruit, that cast a broad shadow over one
side of the yard which her father planted when she
was a child, and as black as the trench water in which
every day of her life she dipped her bucket and took to
the house to wash pans, scrub floors, bathe children.
Auntie Jessica brought a handful of plums and gave
them to me. 'Tek some to Englan and when you see
white man give him and say you Auntie Clarice send
him gift from she back garden in Albion Village, Berbice,
Guyana, South America, all the way across the Ocean,
you hear, and that he and he race must be kind to you
and we, for all body on dis earth is one God's people,
not true?'

Sensing the coming of a lengthy Christian sermon,
my grandfather picked up his churn as a signal of depar-
ture, for Auntie Clarice was famous for her religious
proverbs and parables which she could narrate all day,
recalling passages from the Bible from her voluminous
memory. She reached into her bosom, searched about,
pulled out a handkerchief knotted at one end which she

untied to reveal a five-dollar note creased and humid from being saved up for weeks. She kissed me and put the money in my pocket. As I turned to go she called out a final riddle: 'you is we, remember you is we.' I walked down the village road as puzzled by her outburst as I felt enriched by her money.

We called in at Matam's shop, my grandfather wanting to rest for a while and drink some rum. He borrowed my five-dollar note and ordered a half-bottle for Alfred, Tana and the other men idling around a table waiting for someone to treat them to a drink. They swallowed greedily, wasting Auntie Clarice's money, saved up through weeks of toil, in five minutes. I perched on a stool beside some men slamming down dominoes gleefully or cursing when the play was blocked. Peter came up, went to the bar, ordered a penny mauby. He was my size. I walked off to join him and bought a five-cents sugarcake for myself. Peter was an idiot who, although about eighteen years of age, was stunted in growth of body and mind. Instead of growing tall, he spread sideways, a blubber of fat. He stammered too. People said he fell down a coconut tree when he was a boy, landed on his head and shook up his brain. Peter and I would box for hours under the hot sun surrounded by other boys in the village who spurred us on, taking bets. He would pretend to be Cassius Clay and I would be Sonny Liston. We had heard these legendary names on the radio or from the heated talk of rum-shop men arguing the virtues of one against the other and sometimes nearly coming to blows over the issue. Although Clay beat Liston, I preferred to be Liston because he had spent time in prison for murder, whereas Clay was handsome and nice. I spread my feet like a boxer, pushed out my hand and flashed it at Peter's face. He tried to jog up and down for he heard that Clay danced in the ring, but he was fat and clumsy and could hardly shift his body. Either his feet got tangled up and he threatened to trip over, or else focusing on his feet in the effort to dance meant that he forgot all about his hands, which dangled at his side like excess flesh, and it was easy to hit him repeatedly. The boys squealed with vicious delight when I punched his soft fat body, laughing at him as he shifted stupidly from foot to foot in an uncoordinated dance. Now and again he would remember his hands and push them out at me but he was so slow that I saw his punches coming and easily dodged them, bending and weaving like a real boxer. He advanced towards me and stooped but I hit him before he could continue whatever manoeuvre he was plotting, the blow landing on the socket of his eye, stopping him in his tracks. He stood still, covered his face and began to cry. The boys cackled and booed, rushing up to me and raising my victor's hands high.

Peter was always the first to visit me whenever I arrived in Albion village to spend the holidays. He had never travelled to a town so I was an enthralling figure to him, coming from New Amsterdam. He loved to talk about cricket for which he had a passion. As we wandered about the backdam, he would interrogate me about the game. Rohan Kanhai was an Indian like the two of us, a hunter whose exploits symbolised our own ambitions to triumph, and Peter never tired of my stories about the man.

'Y-Y-You ever see K-K-K-Kanhai bat?'

'Yes,' I lied.

'True, boy you must a-see K-K-K-Kanhai bat,' he said gazing on me with everlasting admiration. As far as he was concerned I came from a place called 'town' where famous cricketers visited and played.

'Is true he does d-d-d-drop on he back and hit f-f-f-four?' he asked.

'All the time,' I answered, picking up a coconut branch and swinging it to imitate Kanhai's special shot as if I had been an intimate and frequent witness of the man's play. He stepped back to get a fuller picture of the stroke, begging me to show him again and again. I did so, getting more accomplished at each attempt so that I could imagine the ball swooshing away to the boundary and the crowds standing up in one unified ovation. 'He does hit six too,' I informed him, picking up a stone and smacking it with the coconut branch into the bush. Peter was amazed.

'Eh boy, how c-c-come the c-c-c-coolie man so strong? Is dhall and r-r-r-rice make he so strong? I h-h-h-hear he fader does cut cane and he mudder sell m-m-m-mango in market,' Peter spluttered in disbelief.

I offered biographical details out of a superior know-ledge, making up stories of how Kanhai grew up on the estate and how, when he was little, he surprised everyone by pulling up a fully grown cane with his bare hands, roots and all, and how he could break the cane with one karate chop, no matter how thick, and how he learnt to swing a bat by watching his father's cutlass raise and chop at all angles, how his father couldn't afford to buy the boy a cricket bat so he used to practise with the cutlass, pretending the cane was a ball and chopping and lashing it for four and six, till the white-man overseer, Mr Bookers himself, noticed him and put up passage money to ship him to England to get coaching with Ted Dexter and Len Hutton and all those world-class players.

Peter gave me some of his mauby to drink and I offered a piece of sugarcake.

'Y-Y-Y-You go meet Kanhai when you go E-E-E-Englan?' he asked in awe.

'Sure, man, I can say hello for you.'

He gave me more mauby as a bribe.

'Tell he to send me he picture and sign he name.' I promised that as soon as I arrived in England I would call in at Lords, contact Mr Kanhai and get him to write a long letter personally addressed to Peter Ramkissoon and send it first-class air mail with a signed photograph of the whole West-Indian team.

My grandfather gathered his goods together, raising the bottle to his mouth and draining the very last drop down his throat. I said goodbye to Peter. We shook hands solemnly like grown-ups. Although I kept company with many village boys, it was Peter who was my closest friend, and the only face and character I remember vividly, several years afterwards in England. Whenever the West Indies tour England and I watch the matches on television I think of Peter, how he would have been beside himself with excitement to have found himself in the stands, in the company of a roaring crowd, seeing before his very eyes the bowler walking towards the pavilion, rubbing the ball on his thigh, turning, setting off slowly at first, working up a pace, the batsman tapping at the crease, waiting, plotting, then, arriving at the mark, roll his arm and hurl the ball with the force of a hurricane towards the wicket. When the bat flashed and the crack of contact echoed around the ground and Peter blubbered, spilt his peanuts and shot up with the whole crowd to catch sight of the ball speeding like a lizard through the grass, two fielders hunting it, but the ball running away, they can't track it, and the crowd wild with passion, clapping or banging soft-drink cans together in spontaneous outbreak of carnival, who then, in the frenzy, would notice Peter, who then would have any interest in jeering him, calling him mad boy, surrounding him and poking sticks at him, screaming 'Peta, Peta/you mother alligata/you sister mosquita/you father run Venezuela'. And Peter would grow fierce, true madness gripping his brain, and he would hit out with fists that were always too slow for them. They broke the circle and scattered in various directions as he trundled off on his fat legs after one of them, stooping to pick up a stone when he realised he would not catch up, and tossing it effetely through the air. The last line in their home-spun calypso referred to the fact that Peter's father had suddenly disappeared one day. He had taken the family's cow out in the morning as normal but neither beast nor man returned that evening. The family waited until late into the night, long after the rum shop had closed and people could be heard stumbling their way homewards through the darkness, until Peter's mother, unable to bear the distress in her heart, lit another lamp and went across to a neighbour to seek help. The neighbour lit his lamp and the two of them went to another house to make enquiries. They went from house to house, calling out to wake up the occupants, and soon there was a large gathering of folk searching the village. My grandmother and I were preparing to go to sleep when through the bedroom window we saw a procession of lamps in the far distance. They were moving along the road towards our house. It was a beautiful sight, like diwali lights flickering in the darkness, little tongues of flame licking and dissolving the night. The lights reached the front of our house, turned down the dam across the canal leading to the yard, stopped, cohered in one large flame and blazed forth as if to burn down the gate. I grew frightened but when I reached for my grandmother she was gone. She had dashed to the verandah where I heard her calling out and the voices answering her. After a series of such exchanges the lights turned and marched up the dam again and she returned to the room.

'Peta Papa gone,' she told me, 'everybody looking for he but de man vanish.' And she tucked me in, blew out the lamp and went next door to wake up my grandfather. I heard them speak but although I pressed my ears against the wall I couldn't make out the words. I heard him get out of bed, and pace up and down the room. Then the back door opened and shut and there was a sound of feet running down the stairs. He must have gone after the lights. My grandmother came back into the room and slipped into bed beside me. She did not hug me as usual but lay wide awake, saying nothing, sighing now and again. I was too excited by the mystery to fall asleep. I tried to stay awake for the morning and it was long after I heard her snoring and the back door slam as my grandfather returned that weariness forced my eyes shut.

Two policemen arrived the next afternoon in the village, getting off Kumar's bus outside the rum shop. Normally Kumar would give people a mere few seconds to disembark, revving up the engine when they were still on the steps to hurry them along. Some people, especially the old folk, would be frightened by the sudden revving noise, clutching their baskets of goods and jumping out quickly, missing a step and tumbling out with their possessions on the roadside. Kumar would grin mischievously, move into gear and shoot off before their curses and damnations, invariably laden with reference to his low-caste ancestry and fatherlessness, could reach his ears. This time, Kumar's bus lingered, and long after the policemen had gone into the rum shop Kumar was still stationary, hoping that they would come out with news which he would transport to the other villages along the road, so that the whole Berbice coast all the way to the border with Suriname would, by nightfall, be apprised of the mystery. Before too long, news of the policemen's arrival spread through our own village and a crowd gathered

46

outside the rum shop, much to Matam's delight, for the sun was fierce and he was plentifully stocked with rum and soft drinks.

The two policemen, after making enquiries of various people in the rum shop, set off for the savannah and bush. A gaggle of small boys trotted after them, eager to participate in the manhunt. Peter, not really understanding that it was his father's life that was imperilled, was as caught up in the excitement as the rest of us. When we all took up sticks he found one too and we all mimicked the policemen before us, probing into the bushes on the way in the hope of sighting a corpse, or pausing to pick things up from the ground as potential clues, inspecting them by turning them over, holding them up to the sun, sniffing them. The policemen threw away everything they picked up but we retrieved them for further examination when we got home and collected many more objects on our own without notifying the policemen in case they merely discredited them. When we reached the pond, they took off their shoes and uniforms and waded in, feeling under the water with their batons. We did the same. Peter, even though he hated the feel of water, stripped off and went in as far as his knees, not daring to go further in case his fat body sank irretrievably in the mud. The rest of us were happy to enter the water and cool off. Some took a running jump, landing with a squeal on their bottoms; others, whilst they were still in the process of pulling off their clothes, their vests over their heads, were pushed in by unseen hands, falling sideways into the water and swallowing mouthfuls, to our great merriment. We splashed about, scooping up mud from the bottom and flinging it on unsuspecting heads, daubing our own faces in it to make silly masks, pulling at other boys' legs as they stood gathering their breath or having a secret pee, so that they fell backwards gurgling for air, and inventing all manner of other games. We forgot the policemen and their purpose, so that when they got out, dressed and walked back sternly to the village, only Peter and a few of the boys followed them, the rest remaining to play until late afternoon in the pond.

The policemen sat in the rum shop relaxing over a bottle, waiting for their bus to take them back to the station. They looked tired and anxious to get back to base but a few drunks kept pestering them with unsolicited information, especially Tana, an ugly, smelly man who practically lived in the rum shop, slumming there from morning until night on the lookout for a free drink. When Matam closed his shop and turned him out late at night Tana would sometimes go around the side, collapse and fall asleep. We did not like him because when his wife sent one of his several children to the rum shop to beg him to come home he would hit the child and chase him away, humiliating the boy before all the big men and making him cry all the way home. Matam felt sorry for the wife and would harness Sheila, a broken-down donkey with patches of skin missing and the edges of her ears chewed off as if victim of life-long bullying. Sheila was exclusively for the service of rum-shop men – they would mount her late at night and make their way home when too much alcohol

48

paralysed their feet. She brayed and groaned under their weight but was sufficiently trained (stickmarks that permanently scarred her sides revealed that much) to persist until the customer reached home. The men frequently fed her rum to see its effects. She would grow excited, kicking at the post to which she was tethered, chewing at the rope and making curious, high-pitched noises. Sheila regularly felt Tana's load on her back. Matam would get two men to lift and position him across her body. She had no need for direction and set off immediately for Tana's house. This would be in daylight, sometimes as early as two in the afternoon, so that the whole village could see Tana being transported home on the donkey, his legs flopping over the sides, and his wife had to quietly endure the shame of it. Sometimes she would come running over to my grandmother's house late at night, her face swollen and hair torn up. My grandmother would pick up a cutlass, go to collect her sister, Auntie Pakul, and the two of them would proceed to Tana's house to abuse him. She would spend the night in the security of Auntie Pakul's house and be taken home the next day when Tana was safely away in the rum shop.

Auntie Pakul was a short stocky woman with huge arms whose husband, also a drunk, had died in mysterious circumstances. They found him hanging from the rafters of the kitchen. People said that Auntie Pakul had strangled him when he was still in an alcoholic stupor and strung him up. People said he was not a man with money troubles, he was never depressed about anything apart from when the liquor was in short supply. He never left a suicide note even though he could read and write a little, so Auntie Pakul must therefore have killed him. She never bothered to deny the rumours by earnest or wailful protestations, and her contentment served to confirm the suspicion in people's minds. She merely buried him somewhere in the backdam and forgot about him, continued to plant her garden and sell once a week in the New Amsterdam market. It was Auntie Pakul who, when she heard that my father had battered my mother, gathered up her vegetables and took the early morning bus to New Amsterdam, arriving a day before her normal time. She would sort out my father in the morning and go and sell her vegetables in the afternoon, catching the late-night bus home after a day of successful dealing. He had returned unexpectedly to New Amsterdam in a rage. He had an office job in the next county, so came home only at the end of the month. Tonight we were surprised to see him, running up to the gate to greet him, but he brushed us aside and stormed upstairs to the bedroom where our mother was resting. We ran after him, sensing trouble, and when we reached the bedroom we could hear her sobbing as he hit her. He had locked the bedroom door so we could not get in. My two sisters, older than me, started to cry, trying the latch frantically. My younger sister and I climbed on the wooden cupboard which housed all our school books, slates, bags and other intimate belongings, and peeped through slits in the bedroom wall to see him pull our mother off the bed by the hair, drag her to a corner out of our sight and beat her. I screamed at him but the voice could not have left my mouth for he continued his blows whilst my two sisters wailed at the sound; my little sister, standing on tiptoe beside me, tried to push her head through the slits to get a better view. We climbed down and moved to the door, desperate but unable to batter it down. His anger eventually ceased and the sound of thumps, my mother stopped sobbing and the girls eased off their hollering. We waited in suspense but could hear nothing. The realisation that she might be dead set off a solitary wail from one of my sisters, but the eldest shouted at her to stop, which she did immediately. I climbed back on the cabinet, peeped through the slits to see her lying strangely on the bed and he naked on top of her, kissing her, and she kissing him back and clasping him tightly. I felt so glad for her, for all of us, a relief so final that it was beyond my own understanding. There was no longer anything to be afraid of, no more a sense of our frailty, no hurt, no sound of crying.

Auntie Pakul arrived when we were in the kitchen eating our breakfast half-heartedly. As soon as she saw my mother's swollen lips she stormed off to the bedroom where my father was still sleeping, shook him awake and without asking any questions cuffed him heavily on the mouth, closed her large hands around his head, as if plucking one of the pumpkins from her garden, and banged it against the wall. We stood at the doorway watching her slap him about the face, not having the slightest desire to intervene. In fact my smaller sister went to the kitchen and brought back the rolling pin so as to arm Auntie Pakul more effectively. I took it away hastily, in case my father saw it and beat her when Auntie Pakul had departed. He cried out that my mother had taken a man when he had gone away, the news had reached him from his brother, but we knew immediately that it was a nasty lie, that his brother was a jumbie good-for-nothing crab-louse low-caste layabout beggerman and cane cutter, and we were glad Auntie Pakul hit him again in the mouth, stopping his accusations. She ordered him out of bed and to pack his clothes right away. She stood around sternly whilst he hauled on his trousers and gathered a few belongings. Constable Gilbert who lived two houses down and who was walking past on his way to work stopped at the gate and shouted when he heard the commotion. Auntie Pakul poked her head through the bedroom window and shooed him away, telling him to mind his own blasted business. When my father was packed, she marched him out of the house to the stelling, put him on the ferry back to where he came from and told him not to return if he wanted to live. We went home to the kitchen, to finish our roti and fried fish with renewed relish.

'Officer, sah, Mr Inspector,' Tana greeted the waiting policemen, saluting drunkenly as he spoke to them, 'tek out your notebook let me tell you who murdered who. One drink, and I solve you case for you and story done.' But the policemen sat impassively, refusing to be drawn into conversation, until he put his hand on the shoulder of one of them in an attempt at friendliness. The policeman slapped it away, his colleague shot up from the bench and growled a rebuke at Tana, pushing him off. He stumbled back and fell to the floor. The other men laughed at him. Tana cursed them all from the floor, not bothering to get up. The biggest crooks in this world, he frothed, are the police. When hooded gangsters with guns batter down people's doors late at night, and take away their jewellery, they are policemen in disguise. They rape young girls in their cells. They carry out executions for the politicians. They will whore their mothers for a bribe. He hawked and spat feebly in their direction, most of the saliva hanging in a ball of slime from his lips. The bus tooted as it approached, the policemen calmly got up and walked out of the rum shop, one of them deliberately stepping on Tana's fingers as he left, mashing in his thick leather boot as if putting out a cigarette.

Peter and I followed them out and headed home, the sound of Tana's howling accompanying us most of the way. Peter was more agitated than usual, stammering heavily, unable to complete any of his sentences and floating from thought to thought. He took out one object at a time from his pocket, from the collection of clues he had gathered on the manhunt, looked at it unintelligently and threw it into the canal which ran the length of the village. By the time we reached his house he had discarded two buttons, one red and one blue, an empty cigarette carton, half a plastic comb, some goat dung hardened into black marbles, a piece of string, four awara seeds and a dead wasp lodged in a leaf. I too emptied my pockets, mostly of brightly coloured pebbles, a strip of rubber from a discarded slingshot, and pieces of lead from some old fish-nets. The clues to his father's existence lay in this jumble which we dumped forever at the bottom of the canal. Peter pushed off the leaf with the wasp on it like a boat, and we stood watching it drift towards the centre, trembling in the fragile ripples. He took up a stone and pelted it in, the wave created tipping the wasp into the water so that fish could nibble at it.

The search for Peter's father was eventually abandoned and the policemen never returned to the village. Many sightings were made, and when word of each one reached the village it aroused a spate of new conversation, new conjectures, which then settled and were forgotten. He was spotted in the capital, Georgetown, either living rough with beggars who blocked the pavements outside the huge Bookers shop, or else was seen pulling up weeds in somebody's front lawn. He was transformed magically into a state of affluence, someone reporting that they glimpsed him in the back of a black speeding limousine like those ridden by Government ministers, all dressed up in a suit and felt hat. Another person swore they saw him perched high at the top of an electricity pole fiddling with the clusters of white generators as if picking coconuts. He was wearing a helmet and Town Council overalls, and his workman's van, crammed with all manner of complicated tools, was parked at the foot of the pole. Yet another claimed to have seen him in a pilot's uniform, stepping out of a car marked British West Indian Airways, accompanied by two beautiful white stewardesses carrying his bags to the reception of the Pegasus Hotel. One person claimed that whilst watching a film at the Victoria Cinema in Regent Street they saw him dressed up like an Indian with feathers on his head and his face marked with war-paint. There was a group of Indians on horseback encircling a wagon of white people and shooting arrows into them. Only one white man and his young yellow-haired wife were left and when Peter's father finally jumped upon her a shot rang out and he staggered, collapsing across her body. He must have been a chief for when he died all the savages suddenly rode away. This latest piece of news set the village boys in a state of excitement for it seemed that Peter's father had become a star-boy in America. Even Peter went about with a new cockiness, plucking up courage to ask the boys to bat, when before, the most they would allow him was to bowl all day under the hot sun whilst they performed all the elegant strokeplay, sending him running repeatedly to retrieve every ball square cut or hooked to the boundary. Nor were the sightings limited to Georgetown. Peter's father cropped up in many parts of Guyana, including the mysterious interior of the country, in a variety of guises: he looked after cows in the company of buck people at a cattle ranch in Lethem; he joined up with a band of black pork-knockers in Essequibo and went off into the bush to find gold; he trapped baby alligators, stuffed them and sold them to the one tourist shop in Atkinson Airport; he grew marijuana in a secret field behind the hills, and took it out late at night in a motorboat to the mouth of the ocean. Peter's father, a small-boned, insignificant peasant who spent all his life in a cow pasture or paddy field, took on legendary proportions, transformed into hero and villain, pioneer, pilot, politician, technician, saviour and beast; those who hardly noticed him now began to dream about him. It was Auntie Pakul, the night before a fire mysteriously gutted her house, destroying all the dollar notes and melting the gold she had saved up over the years in a rice-sack hidden under a loose floorboard, who disclosed to my grandmother that she had dreamt Peter's father was metamorphosed into a firefly, flapping giant wings, which when outspread, cast a black shadow over the earth, and rubbing his feet together could create bolts of lightning – an image that could have come straight out of one of Shaz's record sleeves, except that it was more imaginative in conception – and when Kumar's bus burst a tyre and plunged off the road into the canal drowning three people, my grandmother had previously dreamt Peter's father was caught in the savannah in a rainstorm. His legs trapped in the mud, he called out like a lost calf, but the noise of the thunder and the drumming of rain drowned his cries. But it was also my grandmother who tried to ground the disappearance of the man in everyday reality, saying that it was no wonder he ran away, since all he had was a wife, six daughters who were too young or ugly to marry and a mad boy for a son, enough burden for any man to want to shed. Peter's mother would send him regularly to our house to beg for vegetables or some rice and my grandmother, fed up with doling out charity and often short of food herself, burst out unexpectedly with this explanation, chasing Peter out of the yard empty-handed.

We called on Richilo, my grandfather's brother, to deposit the last of our eggs and milk. We had to walk down a long dam and through some bush before we came to his cabin, a tiny windowless structure with mud walls, a flour-sack hanging over the entrance for a doorway and layers of coconut branches forming the roof. He was sitting on the grass outside the cabin, cross-legged like a Buddha, cleaning the fish he had caught earlier that morning, his hands bloody and messed with bits of fins and entrails. Two basins were before him, one containing fish still flicking in the strong sunlight and excess of air, the other full of neat piles of still and gaping flesh. His hands communicated automatically between basins. Patwa, hurrie, hassa, curass – they came in all hues and shapes. Seizing one, he slit along the belly, and twisting the blade at an angle, scooped out the insides, all in one quick motion. The fish lashed about in his hand, supremely alive in the moment of death. A swift scraping off of scales, gouging out of eyes, and the thing was transferred into the second basin where it lay anonymously among the rest of the disembowelled dead. He breathed in slowly, savouring the rankness which seemed to stimulate his nerves pleasurably, for it quickened the deed of his hands and he worked at a steadily rising pace. My grandfather went up to greet him but I found the stench unbearable and watched from a distance. He was scraping away with the blade as if scraping the skin from his own palm, for the fish was a small flat patwa, barely visible in his open hand. Bit by bit he seemed to be picking and peeling away the skin, indifferent to the pain, perversely self-willed. This, and the sight of black ants swarming around the eyes and pieces of fish gut, made my stomach turn so that I had to sit down. He went into the cabin, came out with a bottle of bush-rum and a calabash shell. He chopped the head clean off a coconut, mixed a cocktail and drank it back, giving the rest to my grandfather. 'Fish, fish, is only fish with hair I want eat,' I heard him shout, laughing at the joke which had become his stale hallmark. He was famous for going about the village on his donkey, blowing wildly on a conch to signal his trade, his basket piled high with fish. He would go up to the young wives, displaying his catch, his breath so reeking with rum and his unwashed body rivalling the stench of the basket that they bartered with him from a distance. 'I gift you all the fish in the oceans of this world,' he would offer poetically and expansively, 'for a sight of your hairy fish,' stretching out his hand for a grope. They did not take offence, having grown accustomed to his drunken vulgarity over the years. Some even half-lifted their skirts as they turned to go back to their kitchens, offering Richilo a tantalising glimpse of thighs, mocking him by their youthful abandon. Richilo laughed, picked up his basket and shouted some parting vulgarity after them, but deep down he felt forsaken. He made his way home miserably, spurring on the donkey with sharp and cruel blows, seeking out the rum bottle as soon as he reached the cabin.

In the rainy season Richilo would seek shelter in my grandmother's house. The rain beat cruelly upon the roof of his hut, washing away the coconut branches, dissolving the mud walls into grey slime. Richilo gathered all his belongings in a rice-sack – cutlass, oil-lamp, fish-net, basket, blanket and bottles of bush-rum – and came to us. He lived in the dark room underneath the house, sleeping among the ripening bananas and tomatoes. He drank every night and cursed at the top of his voice, all manner of obscene utterances. My grandfather missed them all, dead drunk on his bed, but I pretended to be asleep, all the while listening keenly to his outbursts. My grandmother got out of bed and stamped her foot on the floorboards, shouting at him to shut up, but her rebuke only incited him, serving as a challenge to more obscene expressions. 'Jasmattie,' he called out to my grandmother, 'how come you mouth so big, is donkey cock you suck secretly all these years?' Or, 'You pussy skin open wider than Canje swing-bridge, five Bookers ship can pass through one time.' Very few of his outbursts were memorable but the latter curse excited my imagination, for whenever a big ship sailed down the Canje river, a group of us would cycle and gather on the bank to watch the spectacle of the opening of the bridge. It was an ancient iron structure spanning the river, too low for tall ships to pass under. It swung open sideways to let them through, an operation which seemed to take hours,

59

accompanied by massive groans and unearthly shrieks of machinery. Traffic on both sides was held up, and when the bridge swung back into place, some people would go over anxiously, treading softly, in case it suddenly collapsed under them. After Richilo's allusion to it, I could never cross the bridge without a shudder of revulsion and curious guilt.

My grandmother shouted back that he got no shame, how the child sleeping, and tomorrow she go chase he back to the bush, ungrateful bitch, and came back to bed, but I stayed awake in case he turned violent, broke down the door and chopped us to pieces with his cutlass. Some nights, after my grandmother abused him, he would run out of fresh obscenities and shout instead, 'Jasmattie, look out you crab-louse whore I coming for you. Hear how I preparing cutlass to chop off you coconut head.' And he would rub the iron file against his cutlass blade loud enough for us to hear, exaggerating the strokes as he sharpened it. But my grandmother merely threatened to come downstairs and cuff him all the way back to his cabin if he made any more noise, to which he raved out of pride before growing quiet.

'Ma, you not afraid of Richilo?' I asked her out of deep concern one morning as she sat in the yard grating coconut into a basin.

She gave me a piece of copra to chew, dipping it in sugar first. 'No,' she said, 'he is a good man. Is only rum talking.' She continued grating, and when the bowl was full she took a handful at a time, wrapped it in a piece of cloth, twisted until the juice dripped through into a fresh bowl. I took the discarded husk, mixed it with sugar and ate. When I had enough I flung the rest to the fowl, watching them rush up and squabble, pecking frantically at the ground but also at each other.

'Ma, how come Richilo so poor?' I continued questioning, 'how come he live like rat in mud hut?'

My grandmother paused from her labour and sighed as if recalling in her mind the details of Richilo's history. The fowl approached the bowl for more husks. I took a small piece between my fingers and held it out. They stopped, cocked their heads, looked up at me warily, but none of them were courageous enough to take it from my hand. I put it back in the bowl with a flourish to let them see that I was in control of all the food and that only total obedience to me would yield rewards. They shifted uneasily, looking up, pecking at their feet, looking up again. One or two ventured closer, but at the slightest shift of my hand they moved back in a panic, unsure as to whether I was going to feed them or shoo them away.

'And who would believe the man once had shoe on he foot and walk this world like royalty,' she suddenly blurted out, awakening from her dream and breaking some fresh copra.

'Which man?' I asked, 'which foot?' so distracted by playing with the birds that I had forgotten my original question.

'Shoe mind you, not rubber slipper but brown leather with shiny buckle, and cork hat cock-up on his head like lover-boy film star. Prince Richilo!'

'Richilo was a prince?' I asked incredulously, excited by a sense of unfolding drama, 'Richilo a prince?' I suddenly remembered the Indian films I had seen in the Globe Cinema, and Richilo's story immediately made sense without further explanation from my grandmother. He must have been a great man, a rich handsome young man full of song and colour, a garland of flowers around his neck, living in a large white concrete house, with three floors and a fountain in the garden, servants at the door, in the kitchen, in the hall, some polishing the gold ornaments, others playing music on stringed instruments whilst he moved among them singing, dancing, springing on the sofa, off the sofa, kneeling on the carpet, arms outspread and song pouring from his mouth, leaping up again, twirling, running to the door, followed by a troupe of servants who were also singing; stopping, turning, running back into the hall, taking all the servants with him until, at the climax of the song, they held him aloft in one movement, triumphant, regal, and all of us in the pit of the Globe, enraptured by the music, the sumptuous wealth and the costumes, rose up with him, our minds soaring from the wooden benches, lifted from the rough concrete with its puddles of urine which some of us made, not wanting to miss a minute of film, not wanting to leave the cinema to relieve ourselves in the trough outside. India was full of princes like Richilo who, forsaken by lovers, spurned by potential brides, or infatuated with beautiful but forbidden Muslim women (if they were Hindu and vice-versa) or servant girls, lost control of their lives, neglected their businesses and died in wretchedness; their once-loyal servants stole from them, betrayed them, fed them poison.

'Is rum. All you Pa family is rum-suckers,' my grandmother continued, 'low-breed coolie people who bring they bad habit all the way from India.' And she sucked her teeth in contempt.

'India is far?' I asked Ma. 'How far India stay from here? Far? And Richilo prince for true?' But it was getting late, there were pots to be scrubbed and the half-drum of fresh water in the kitchen needed replenishing. She got up, put away the bowls of coconut milk and went off to the village well.

I lingered in the yard with nothing to do and no one to talk to. I went to lie down in the hammock, waiting for my grandfather to come through the yard with the cows, the final flurry of activity which signalled the end of the day. He would secure the cattle in their pens, wash the mud from his feet, his stick and cutlass and go upstairs to dish out his dinner of curry and rice. He would sit on the verandah with his enamel plate and eat rapidly, scooping food to his mouth in a series of continuous movements, sucking and chewing and spitting out bones. From the hammock I could see malabunta wasps busily making nests on the eaves of the verandah roof, large grey lanterns which, when they became too plentiful, my grandfather would destroy with his magic stick. He tied a rag soaked in kerosene to the top of his stick, lit it, reached for the nests and set fire to them one by one. A week later a small bud would appear, occupied by two or three new wasps, which gradually grew to a lantern and multiplied into more lanterns. They flew in and out in ceaseless unfathomable activity, until my grandfather burned them at the end of the month.

She came back with the bucket of water poised on her head. I got up and followed her to the kitchen, watching her stoke the fireplace with fresh wood and light it. She let me blow through a piece of iron pipe to encourage the flames. The kitchen filled with blue dreamy smoke. I left her tending pieces of fish and a pot of boiling rice and went back to the hammock. My grandfather shook me awake and took me upstairs on his back, depositing me on the verandah. It was the last hour of light. A flock of rooks were flying home in formation and other birds, blue sakis and kiskadees, followed in loose numbers, all heading in one procession across the sky. From the verandah I could see into the yards of the houses in the neighbourhood. Each had a fowl-coop, a cow pen and a vegetable patch. Apart from the livestock the yards were empty. Everybody was indoors cooking or eating. My grandfather returned with two plates of curry.

'Pa, how come Richilo so poor?' I asked, 'what happen to all he servants?'

My grandfather stuffed his mouth, chewed and sucked the chicken bones before spitting them out over the verandah rails. He was too hungry and tired to talk. After eating he fished out a bottle of rum from his back pocket and swallowed half of it. When he heard my grandmother approach with two mugs of black tea he slid it quietly back into his pocket. He took the empty plates and cups and went off to the kitchen, leaving me by myself on the verandah. The darkness came swiftly and the noise of crappaud which had been building up in the half-light reached a pitch of frenzy. Lamps were lit one by one all over the village. Rain began to fall suddenly, as if signalled by the flames, beating loudly on the zinc roof and drowning the call of the crappaud. The gate rattled and Richilo trudged through the mud with his sack of belongings on his back. I heard him moving about in the room downstairs, cursing as he stumbled in the darkness.

'Is rum,' Ma confided in me that night as I lay alongside her in bed, but she fell asleep before I could discover more.

We left Richilo's hut laden with fish and coconuts and headed home. It had been a successful morning's trade. My grandfather, light-headed with rum, swayed unsteadily down the mud dam leading to the village road. He was in a happy mood. When we reached the house, he put away the churn and coconuts and gave my grandmother the fish and most of the money. He took the cows to the savannah. 'When you coming back boy?' he asked as he left, not waiting for an answer. My grandmother went off to fetch more water. I lay in the hammock watching her daub the bottom-house with fresh mud and manure, covering over the cracks. She worked all morning at several tasks simultaneously. Whilst food was cooking on the fireside she chopped up firewood for another day. She rinsed out clothes and hung them on the verandah rails to dry. She swept the hall. She fed the hens. She brought me a piece of fried fish to the hammock. She ironed the clothes as soon as they were dry. She swept the rest of the house. She counted out money and went to Matam's shop to buy salt and flour. I followed her knowing that on this my last day she would treat me with sweets and Matam's wife's homemade cakes.

'Old Juncha come from India long-time,' she said, 'last century,' and pointed out a stone post half-buried in shrub, set back from the road, a few yards from Matam's shop. I had never noticed it before. When we reached it she sent me to brush aside the weeds and read it.

'"New Amsterdam 60 miles",' I shouted after her, for she had continued walking towards the shop.

'That stone plant there in old Juncha day, the same stone on he grave in St Ann churchyard. He turn Christian and get bury with hymn and preacher man and all.'

I wondered who old Juncha was, and why she was telling me this story. Whilst she bought goods from Matam I ate a roly poly and drank a bottle of Pepsi, feeling rich in the company of stray boys who lingered eternally around Matam's shop, with nothing to do but play bat-and-ball, beg people coming and going from the shop for pennies to buy sweets, all the time waiting to grow up when they could then join the company of rum drinkers in the bar section of the shop. I ate another cake, this time an expensive currant bun and was given another drink, a Seven-Up, the latest pop in the country. The boys gathered around, awed by my privilege, but my grandmother shooed them off. As we left the shop, Matam uncorked a bottle filled with toffees and gave me a handful as a gift to take to England. The sight of Matam actually giving away sweets was the most astonishing event of the year for the small boys, for Matam was notoriously mean to small boys. No matter how much they begged, or promised to weed his yard or wash out the empty bottles, Matam would not budge, would not part with toffees. He had four glass jars perched high on a shelf, out of reach of small thieving hands, stuffed with sweets in all colours.

'Englan far away like India,' my grandmother said as we made our way home. I was too bloated with food and gas from the soft drinks to care where England was. India too was unimaginably far, too far to bother with. She sensed my torpor and stopped talking.

'Juncha was Richilo's grandfather,' she continued after a while, baiting me with the mystery.

I awoke partially. 'Ma, why Richilo so poor?' I asked automatically for the umpteenth time over the years, and this time she unfolded a confusing tale about Juncha, Richilo's grandfather, my great-great-grandfather, who came from India in a boat with a dhoti wrapped around his waist and a sack of belongings on his back. He came to cut cane and was bound for five years to plantation Canje. He was lazy at first, as if the work was below his dignity, but two sudden stick-lashes on his back from the white man soon set him chopping crazily in the cane field. By the time his indenture had expired he had amassed enough money by mysterious processes to buy a portion of an abandoned cotton plantation from the white owner, some fifty acres of land on the east side of Albion Village on which he kept cows and traded in meat and grew fat on the profits of his cunning. Some said he had acquired his original fortune by theft, but as there was little to steal from the plantation apart from the odd bundle of cane and timber and tools from the overseer's house, no one could identify the precise nature of his illegal business. Others claimed that he had discovered in the cane field a hoard of gold buried by white adventurers and pirates centuries before and had sold it piece by piece over the five years. Many put it down to Indian witchcraft, for although he had converted to Presbyterianism to benefit from the patronage of missionaries and to win the favour of the overseer, he would nevertheless disappear from time to time in the bush where, it was said, he sacrificed a lamb, feeding the blood to the root of a special tree which housed a snake which he had brought all the way from India wrapped around his waist and hidden under his shirt. It was a god-snake which blessed him with fortune for his devoted worship. Juncha prospered on his plantation and married a fair-skinned girl from a higher caste who bore him five sons. He ruled the village in a display of benevolence, presiding at baptisms, marriages and deaths, disbursing alms to the beggars, buying wood to build a Scots church, supervising the work on it and fêting the catechists who came from town on several weekends to spread the Gospel. A few envious Indians spoke sullenly about his ill-gotten wealth, reminding people that he was an ex-canecutter from disreputable, low-caste ancestry, a jumped-up coolie with a magic snake. But they were afraid to talk too loudly in case Juncha turned the deity against them. He ignored them, sitting prominently on his verandah all day reading the Bible and eating from a bowl of Indian sweets which a boy servant kept filling up periodically. He had hired hands to look after his growing herd of cattle. Each Friday, to the disgust of Hindu and Muslim alike, he slaughtered a cow and pig in a specially constructed shed, hacking them to pieces and taking the meat in a cart to the neighbouring village to sell to black people.

Hundreds of people from all over the countryside congregated in his yard when Juncha died, some out of sorrow, the rest out of mere curiosity. He had a loud and splendid funeral, a dozen hymns were sung and the priest, a red-skinned negro from New Amsterdam, bellowed out a sermon through a megaphone. Refreshments were provided in abundance, enough to feed the village for a month, for it was Juncha's will that he should be remembered with gratitude. A wagon pulled by four black horses paraded his coffin along the village road. It was a day of excitement and pageantry mingled with wailing from Juncha's wife. They buried him in a graveyard beside the church. His gravestone was massive, dwarfing the others, with lettering carved on it which few could read. His family stayed on in the graveyard, planting a flower bed, erecting an iron railing around the mound, but the less concerned, after paying their perfunctory respect, headed back to the yard to finish off the food.

The five sons quarrelled with each other, partitioned the land and built individual houses. Their children in turn inherited a portion, so that by the time of Richilo's generation, each of Juncha's male offspring possessed no more than a vegetable garden. Juncha's grand spread had shrunk to minute patches, even as he was reduced from fat flesh to pieces of dry bone. People forgot the grandeur of the man and the substantial proportions of his original purchase of land. In the divisions and sub-divisions all the markers defining the expanse of land were forked over. His gravestone became covered over with green slime which hid the lettering proclaiming the glory of his life, so that for all their increased literacy the successive generations still could not read it.

'So Ma, man, how come Richilo so poor?' I asked impatiently for the final time, but we had reached home and she automatically resumed her work, hurrying away to the kitchen to tend the pots, forgetting me.

When the time came, after I had eaten and bathed and dressed in freshly ironed clothes and before my grandfather returned from the savannah, she and I awaited wordlessly by the roadside for the noise of the horn. 'Go and don't look back,' she said, putting me on Kumar's bus back to New Amsterdam at the end of the last day, 'or else Albion ghosts go follow you all the way to Englan.' She pinned a tiny gold brooch on my shirt, inscribed with my initials, gathered up the two bags of my belongings and gifts I had received from the villagers earlier in the day and shoved me in without a kiss, throwing the bags after me. Kumar roared the engine and screeched off and when I found a seat by the window and looked back she had gone. I sat quietly, not noticing anyone, hugging the two bags, the water coconuts that Richilo had given me bulging out of one of them and threatening to roll away on the floor out of reach.

II

OUR SUMMER HOLIDAY job was simple, exhilarating and extremely profitable. At eight a.m. Shaz and I arrived at Battersea Fun Fair, and prepared the World Cruise for the day's pleasure seekers. The act of putting on the uniform provided by the proprietor always gave us a feeling of authority and responsibility: we were part of a community of artistes, showmen, technicians and businessmen and we were in sole charge of the World Cruise ride. Shaz's first task was to collect a roll of numbered tickets and a bag of coins from the office. He signed his name at the bottom of a sheet, always with a flourish, and underlining it with two gay strokes of the pen as if he were signing the richest cheque in the world. I collected a long aluminium rod with a hooked end to pull the boats along when they got stuck in the canal. Shaz took up his position in the booth, placed his roll of tickets in the dispenser and laid out the coins on the shelf, in neat piles of pennies and shillings. Then he switched on the microphone, cleared his voice, and practised his call: 'World Cruise! World Cruise! Austria to Zanzibar, adventure of a lifetime!' He fancied himself a rock star, clutching the microphone and grunting a line of lyric, until the proprietor, Mr King, threatened to dismiss him if he did not take his job seriously.

The fairground was cranking up for the day's excitement. All around us were stall-holders, busily arranging coconuts, fluffy toys, teddy bears and other prizes for the crowd. The Ghost Train next door rehearsed its ride, rattling round its track, banging into doors, sweeping through plastic cobwebs, confronting grinning skeletons before emerging into sunlight again. Horses on the merry-go-round were awakened and put through their paces, bobbing up and down to the sound of fiddles. Helicopter blades whirred in anticipation of screaming children. The one-armed bandits had their glass faces wiped and were fed a few preliminary coins. Pennies would be pressed into their mouths all day until their insides groaned with copper. Every two hours or so the owner would come along and the bandits relieved themselves into his collecting bag.

At 8.15 I switched on the lights and the motor which made artificial waves, sending boats floating downhill through the tunnel and into the realms of the picturesque and fantastic. The tunnel wall was decorated with painted scenes from various countries, in alphabetical order. These pictures were lit with special red lamps so that they glittered in a magical way. When the lights were switched off the pictures lost their fascinating glow and when I shone an ordinary torch on them I could see only smears of paint, crude in composition, lacking in artistry and beauty. My first task was to fish the cans and plastic bags out of the water, tossed there by the previous day's throng. I had a special net to scoop these out, as well as the scum of decaying popcorn and crisps that collected at various turnings of the canal. The World Cruise attracted lovers, not so much because of the spectacular exhibitions but the relative darkness of the tunnel and the length of the ride, some fifteen minutes from beginning to end, in which they could obviously cast off superfluous clothing. On some mornings I would collect an assortment of underclothing, male and female, abandoned between Fiji and Timbuktu, two minutes into the ride and two minutes from the exit. I stood on the prow of my boat, torch in one hand, spiked aluminum rod like a fearsome weapon in the other, the artificial ventilation blowing back my hair, gliding down the canal in quest of debris. I flowed past Austria in natural light, for it was at the very mouth of the tunnel, and nodded familiarly to the man on the snow-capped mountain-top dressed in rustic jacket, half-trousers, long woolly socks, a curious cap, who had his mouth eternally at a long horn. At the foot of the mountain was a church and the suggestion of a pretty village. It had a shop full of dolls, all pink-cheeked and pristine, sitting with open legs on a shelf. Past Austria, the boat was enveloped in darkness, the air not so much brooding and mysterious as dank and still, the smell of unclean water filling my nostrils. I sat down to enjoy the strange images beaming from the walls, my net slowly filling up with a bounty of gleaming tin, popcorn like pieces of dissolved pearl, lumps of gold-coloured toffee wrappings. When the boat passed Greece I looked out for Guyana, but the proprietors had neglected us and took us straight to India instead. There I paused by sticking the rod against the wall to admire the gorgeous Taj Mahal, its domes soaring to a sky lit by a crescent moon, and a stunning Indian princess, wrapped in a white sari, attended by hand-maidens as she strolled through a garden of flowers, a tiger cub walking on a lead before her. There was a sadness in her eyes, as if all the fragrances of the garden and of her body, and the innocence of the maidens, were threatened by the black crow perched on the garden gate. The crow was obviously sinister. Not only was it blocking the way, but the artist had emphasised the length of its claws and its long curved beak like an oriental dagger. The scenes of Timbuktu by contrast, were depicted in harsh sunlight. There was a desert, some scorched trees, and five naked black men squatting or throwing spears after a zebra. They wore necklaces made out of the teeth of animals and each had a bone running through his nostrils. A black woman with full breasts and gleaming thighs carried a pot on her head. Another sat on a donkey so oddly – her buttocks merged into its flank – that it seemed she was having some kind of bizzare sex with it.

Someone had scrawled 'niggers out' on her body and had drawn a fat penis pointed at her mouth. The genitalia of the black men had also been elongated or smudged as if to erase them. I dipped a rag in the water and wiped out the marks as best I could, feeling silly as

I worked on the private parts of the men and relieved that there was no one to see me rubbing all over the woman's body.

The journey ended, the next task was to clean the boats. This was an adventure in itself, for invariably one found a few coins that had slipped out of people's pockets and wedged themselves in odd corners. Because we were schoolboys the owners paid us only a small sum but we increased this by a simple trick. When a ticket was sold, the fun-seeker brought it to me. I had to tear it in two, return one half to him and lead him to a boat. The other half I stuck on a piece of wire. But the two of us worked a system whereby I did not bother to tear the ticket, especially when the purchaser was a child or a foreigner, unsure of the procedure. I merely pocketed the whole ticket, and as soon as the boat set off I returned the ticket to Shaz for him to re-sell. We had to be very alert to the comings and goings of the owner, as he collected the takings and the torn tickets periodically throughout the day, but after a while we were able to time his routine to the minute. By this method we made ten shillings or so per day, which we shared out as soon as work was over and we were safely on the bus to Balham.

I always gave Shaz the larger share, for it was he who got me the job in the first place and found me a room in which to live after I had left the Home. It was a choice between staying in the Boys' Home run by the Social Services and finding a place of my own. The Home was in fact a prison for youth, and the innocent who were taken there were soon converted to criminal ways. Boys abandoned by parents through no fault of their own quickly grew into little gangsters. On the first day they came in shyly, with a suitcase of poor belongings, accompanied by a social worker. The natives, some of whom had been living there as long as they could remember, scooted along the corridors, screaming and throwing things at each other. One was practising karate against the wall, chopping at it in an imaginary act of brick-breaking. A ball shot out by an invisible foot slammed against a door, ricocheted against another, tumbled down the main stairs and rolled to the reception desk where the newcomer, petrified, waited to be signed in. The boy expected at any moment a horde of youths to charge down the stairs in pursuit of the ball and he made preparations to shift out of the way, noting the distance between himself and the exit in case he had to make a run for it, but no one followed to retrieve the ball. The foot that had kicked it off was busy kicking at something else.

The man at the desk was nice. 'Call me Cyril,' he said, smiling broadly, 'tea is at five o'clock in the dining room. Shout if you need help.' He was totally careless of the pandemonium around him, whistling softly as he wrote down things in the boy's file and put it away in the cabinet. The boy collected the key and he and his social worker made their way to his room. The social worker poked his head in to make sure all the statutory items were present and correct – a bed, a chair, a desk, a wardrobe – muttered a few words about good behaviour or good luck, closed the door and disappeared for ever. The boy sat on the bed, unsure about what to do. Although he had passed a few of the inhabitants along the corridor, no one appeared to have noticed him. He unpacked his clothing, which took no time at all, and sat on the bed again, waiting for someone to knock. No doubt someone would come in to say hello and to show him around the place, introduce him to a few of the other boys. He waited, but no one came, and being too afraid to venture out, and in any case not quite knowing what to do once he got to the other side of the door, he remained on the bed. He wondered where the toilets were.

The Home was unbearable. Of the fourteen boys, there were nine white, four black, and myself. Apart from Joseph, one of the blacks, the rest were impenetrable. They had a system of gangs between them, so that not until the newcomer had graduated through a period of seasoning could he be drawn into one alliance or another and set to work on theft, vandalism or some other criminal pursuit within and outside the Home. Joseph was different. He arrived suddenly in my third year at the Home, having been transferred from a borstal in Bethnal Green, and before that from a succession of welfare hostels all over London. Although rumours soon spread about his dangerous past, Joseph showed no signs of criminal life. Day and night, it seemed, he sat at the window strumming a guitar and singing to himself. I wondered whether he was related to the guitar man in New Amsterdam who lived opposite us. It was a small house on stilts, and the black man lived under the house, in the open, with a hammock strung between the stilts as his bed. There was a small table and a wooden box in which he kept his possessions. His mother, an elderly woman in grey plaits, lived upstairs by herself, and whenever it was time to eat she came down with a plate of food for him. When it rained, and the bottom-house was flooded, she led him upstairs with his guitar. As soon as he woke up he reached for his guitar and began to play. He was a madman, but harmless to children; when we paused on the road on our way to school to listen to him he was oblivious to us, his head bent to the strings and his fingers moving up and down. Now and again he would lift his head and stare at us without really seeing, his hand still working at the strings. We were a little afraid of him on account of his madness but a few bold ones, including myself, ventured into the yard to get a closer look at his method of playing. We were enchanted by the music, for it was unimaginable that we could ever possess a guitar. We marvelled at the fact that a madman could play such a thing. Once, after he had rested it carefully on the table and gone off to urinate against one of the stilts, I ran my fingers against the strings to produce a thrilling sound. I could see my face in the sheen of the wood. It was the first time that I had ever touched a musical instrument. When he came back I withdrew my hand hurriedly and retreated a few paces, preparing to scoot off, but he was not in the least bothered, merely taking up his guitar and resuming his play. This lack of intimidation took me by surprise and made me feel a sudden friendship for him, so that every afternoon when I returned from school I would go into the yard, sitting down on the table to listen to him with the growing attentiveness and respect of a disciple. Of course he never noticed me but I felt there was a kindness between us nevertheless, a knowledge that he was tolerant of my presence and that I was captivated by the sounds he made. I never imposed upon this unspoken friendship and never again attempted to touch his guitar when he laid it down and went away.

'I have to make something of my life and move out of this place,' I told Joseph, 'that is why I work at my essays.' He had wandered into my room and remarked upon the books scattered on the bed and desk. He picked up a history text and flicked through it, looking at the pictures.

'What do you do?' he asked, and when I said I was studying for my 'A' levels I had to explain what these were, for it had been a few years since he had attended school. No one seemed to bother to ensure his attendance, certainly not Cyril who was permanently sitting in his office, watching television or reading the newspapers.

'I can't read or write,' he said, looking up from the book to get my reaction.

I was in the middle of a paragraph of Conrad's *Heart of Darkness* and wished he would go away. The sound of his guitar when he was in the next room was soothing, inspiring me to think and write in bursts of creativity, but to have him before me was exasperating, given that I had to hand in the essay the next morning.

'What these pictures about then?' he asked childishly, holding up the history book.

'The Second World War,' I snapped, not looking up, trying to recover and re-shape an idea he had disturbed by coming into my room.

He studied the pictures. 'What is that you reading?' he asked again after a while, pointing to the novel held in my hand.

'It's another book,' I answered automatically, putting pen to paper, but knowing that the effort was futile. Before he could ask what it was about, I spun round, intending to ask him to leave until I had finished the essay. He could come back then and I would go through each of the twenty books if necessary and explain all their secrets. His face was buried in the history book, the Rastafarian locks hanging untidily on either side of the covers.

'I know him,' he blurted out, his eyes gleaming with discovery as they lifted from the page, and he thrust the book at me, pointing to a picture of Winston Churchill. 'My father had a big photo of him in his workshop. Who is he?'

'He won the war,' I said.

'Which war?' he wanted to know.

'The last one,' I told him, 'and the one before that, and the one before that. He won all the wars that England fought, they're all the same. It's only that the last one was the biggest, all the rest were leading up to that one.'

He was fascinated and I was struck by my own wisdom. The overview I had given him suddenly appeared to make sense of all the scattered epochs we were studying for the history 'A' level. I saw in a flash of intuition how even the Conrad was integrated into the total picture, but before I could pin the idea down on the page with the tip of my pen he started to talk again about Churchill's photograph.

It must have been his father I met many years later by total accident in another part of the land when Joseph was all but forgotten in my mind. I was driving through Birmingham going somewhere or other, when my engine cut out. A passer-by told me of a garage further up the road. I locked the car and wandered through the slums in search of help, passing tower block after tower block, until I came to a ramshackle aluminium shed surrounded by the skeletons of abandoned cars. There was a strong smell of petrol. An old man was inside, his head lowered into the bonnet of a van. He grunted when I called out, but continued to work at the belly of the vehicle, ripping out pieces of wire, prising out nuts. After a while he looked up. His face was stained with engine oil, a screwdriver poked out from a tuft of hair, and a chain of spanners hung from his neck. I told him what the problem was. It would take him at least two hours before he would be able to start on my car. When I bribed him with extra money he abandoned his work on the van and set off with a tool box to find my car. I idled about the workshop, waiting for his return. Pieces of machinery were scattered hopelessly on the floor, and I began to wonder whether the man was a skilled mechanic or a modern cannibal, whether my car would be dismantled beyond the point of recovery. My eyes roved over the carcass of the van and alighted suddenly on a photograph of Winston Churchill upon the far corner of the shed. It was neatly framed and the glass was surprisingly clear, given the quantity of grease and oil smeared all over the walls. It was the cleanest object in the shed, as if special care was lavished to protect it from the hazards of the workshop.

When he returned eventually with the car, I asked him about the picture but he merely grunted and buried his head under the bonnet of the van.

'What was the matter with it?' I asked, trying to strike up a conversation so that I could put to him the intimate question of his fatherhood.

'Nothing,' he growled, 'spark plug seize up.'

'Thanks a lot for all your help,' and as I turned to go, I called out Joseph's name. 'Any relation to you?'

'Joseph who?' he asked, raising his head to find a hammer. He banged at the engine.

'I can't remember another name,' I shouted above the din. My words must have been drowned by the hammer blows for he did not look up again. I lingered for a moment, caught between a sudden melancholy and a desire to investigate, then drove off.

'About six years,' he estimated vaguely when I asked him how long he had lived in Homes. He wasn't sure how old he was either, seventeen or thereabouts. They would turn him out when he was eighteen and he would either go to prison or find a place for himself. He wasn't bothered, he said. And what about me? How come I liked books so much? What would I do when I grew older? Where did I come from? I had nothing interesting to say to him, much preferring – when time permitted – to listen to his stories, especially his scrapes with authority. He had spent much time in borstals and police cells for crimes exclusively related to cars, vandalising parking meters, joy-riding, stealing mascots, smashing the car windows and helping himself to car radios, money from glove compartments, packages in the back seats. All that was behind him, he said, for he had become Rastafari and all he wanted to do was to learn black history and spread love and feelings to everybody.

'Even when I used to thieve I never hurt nobody, I never rob nobody's pocket. I never hit nobody in their face or molest them. Is only youth, and anyway, the little something I take from cars is no bank robbery or cause grievous injury to nobody.'

'So why,' I asked, 'do you think you will go back to prison?'

He looked at me as if I was born yesterday.

'How you mean? If you talk peace, they think you only smoking weed. Is a dangerous thing to preach feelings and oneness. They prefer you to hang around cars.'

I could not really get to know him to begin with, not only because I moved out of the Home soon after he arrived, but because he had a way of rambling, never getting to the point. When I asked him about his parents for example, I had to endure about ten minutes of waffle before I could discover that his mother died early of some disease in England and that his father had moved north somewhere, having put him in an orphanage. He lacked precision in everything, unable to remember a year, a name, an episode. He organised his life totally around a vague ambition to give love to people. It did not seem to matter that no one wanted to receive it or appreciate any nobility in him. The other boys thought him strange and unrealistic, especially since he refused to impart his criminal knowledge to them.

That he was skilled in all manner of survival was brought home to us after he had broken out of jail. How he did so was beyond our comprehension, for when Shaz and I visited him in his hideout, he gave vague answers to our questions, as if picking locks and climbing over walls was so self-explanatory that he could not be bothered to go into details. He had phoned to tell us where he was, and we went immediately to his aid, carrying a plastic bag stuffed with crisps, apples and lemonade. It was an abandoned house in a Balham back-street, in a row of derelict buildings. His face was swollen with bruises, but his only worry was that the police had taken away his video camera forever. He was desperate to recover it, and was even contemplating breaking into the police store-room where they had locked it up pending enquiries.

Shaz and I felt responsible for his distress for it was

the two of us who had put the idea of film-making into his head. Shaz, desperate to learn to play the guitar, was a frequent visitor to the Home, and whilst the two of them made curious noises next door I scribbled away at my essays.

'I must get out of this place,' I said one evening, bursting into Joseph's room, 'it's a mess, I can't concentrate.'

Shaz was too busy to bother with me, trying out a new three-fingered trick that Joseph was teaching him. He gripped the guitar clumsily and his fingers kept slipping from the neck, which Joseph kept correcting. When he eventually got it right and strummed with his hand, an ugly noise escaped and he became agitated and disappointed. Even Joseph was surprised by the unexpected sound; he took the guitar from him and tried it out, producing a gentle melody. He gave it back to Shaz, stood over him, helping him to position his fingers on the strings, and when everything was in place instructed him to begin again. Shaz strummed, but the noise was terrible. Joseph, patient as ever, rearranged Shaz's fingers but in spite of all his coaching, Shaz could not entice a single melodious chord from the guitar.

'It take time,' Joseph comforted him, himself puzzled by the dissonance, for as soon as he took the guitar up, put his fingers at the exact places where Shaz had positioned his and strummed, music flowed.

'Perhaps you got no soul for the instrument, you gotta let your feelings press into the strings,' he concluded, but Shaz scowled. 'Think of children on a swing,' he said, going off at a tangent in search of the right meta-phor. He had a gift of coming up with comparisons that came very close to the mark but finally shot past by a mile. 'If they not feeling anything, just sitting there all glum then there is no life in a swing, you know. They not getting anywhere. They might as well be sitting on a park bench or rooftop. They've gotta push hard on the ground and swing back high and giddy and ripple all excited, and the music burst in their heart.'

'I don't want to break my neck in a playground, all I want is to play a few chords on this bloody guitar, what stupidness you on about?' Shaz retaliated.

'That is because you got no vision,' Joseph replied softly.

'What has that got to do with it?' Shaz continued, 'it's a simple matter of getting your fingers in the right places.'

'That's 'cause you can't see,' Joseph argued, 'and if you can't see you can't play, for your whole body block up with darkness so there is no light in your soul to guide your fingers.' He spun an erratic parable about a blind man stumbling along a rocky road, bumping into things, cursing and crying out in pain. 'The point is,' he concluded at last, 'the rock blind as well, but it stay forever in one place if necessary, for all time if necessary, not moving. Why? Because if it move in its blindness, it would bump against the man and bruise him up and hurt him. So is the blind man who at fault and causing self-pain and injury to the rock. He should be patient and be all compose like the rock and wait for guidance before he set off.'

He was in the middle of telling us how rocks had life, how Moses brought forth the water of life by touching the rocks in divine guidance, when Shaz got up to go in frustration. 'Look,' Joseph interrupted him, and he took up the guitar, closed his eyes and played a melody. 'No eyes, you don't need them if you got vision or guidance.' His fingers slid in mysterious formations over the strings. Even Shaz was arrested by the ease and gracefulness of their movements. 'You try,' he said, offering Shaz the guitar and urging him to be guided by his soul. But it was no good, Shaz refused to close his eyes and appear foolishly mystical. He desperately wanted to play the guitar with the intensity of Carlos Santana. He knew that Joseph was right about the element of mysticism, but he was too self-conscious to engage with it openly.

'I must get out of that place,' I muttered grumpily to Shaz as we wandered from shop-window to shop-window reading the advertisement cards. Shaz was in a frivolous mood though. It was all right for him – he had a spacious room in his parent's house and all his needs were provided for by his mother who ironed his clothes and cooked for him. His father gave him five pounds a week pocket money, so he could afford to buy trendy shirts and shoes. I was getting shabbier by the day.

'Black Beauty offers V.I.P. massage to kind gents in comfort of her own house. Cleanliness assured and demanded,' he read out. His laughter could not disguise a nervous excitement.

'Come on, man,' I barked at him, 'either you help me or don't bother.'

He sulked and turned back to the board of cards, scrutinising it for lodgings on offer. 'No one will rent you a room because you don't have money and you are only sixteen. People don't rent rooms to kids.'

I knew that already, but it was hopeless trying to find accommodation in a white household. My best bet was to locate an Asian landlord and it was for this reason that I had asked Shaz to accompany me, for he at least could speak the odd word in one or two Asian languages. The only cards I paid attention to were those which suggested an Asian landlord. This was a matter of chance for the cards rarely carried the names of landlords, only telephone numbers. The only clues to ethnicity were in mis-spelt words or handwriting that evidenced a struggle to come to terms with a new language; but even these were no guarantee, for the whites themselves could be astonishingly illiterate in English.

'Here's one,' I cried, pulling out a pen to scribble the number in the palm of my hand.

'Definitely Paki,' he offered after studying it.

It was certainly a semi-literate scrawl, and in green ink, the national colour of Pakistan, and the number suggested the Asian quarter of Balham, though the whole of Balham was in any case becoming Asian territory. 'Room to lett big house going cheape for person working 6727067 anytime or call round, 296

Cherry Road, anytime.' Before setting out that morning I had polished my shoes and ironed my shirt and trousers, in preparation for meeting landlords. I had a ten-pound note in my pocket, the totality of my personal wealth, to put down as a deposit. I was determined to escape the Home.

Mr Ali answered the door wearing white pyjamas and chewing pan and betel-nut. After long negotiation in broken English and Urdu he showed us to a tiny room containing a bed, a set of drawers, a table and chair. He said he did not let without references. There were four rooms in his house all occupied by decent professional people, and he wanted to keep things spick and span. When would I be paying? Who would give him the money? Did he have to sign forms with the Social Services? Did he have to fill out a tax return? He did not like paperwork or any trouble from the authorities. I had better look elsewhere for a room. Dozens of people wanted the room, and he had to give it to the most suitable candidate, what else could he do, he was sure we would understand his predicament. He had a large mortgage to pay; he could not afford to take pity on anyone. Shaz and I answered his queries and objections as best we could and he lowered his guard as soon as I displayed my ten-pound note. 'I will give you another ten-pounds on the day I move in,' I offered, thinking it best to make a firm promise now and worry later how to produce the money. Again he softened his attitude and before we left he offered us some tea, continuing to probe into my background, anxious to ensure that he got paid and at the same time feeling sorry for someone of his own race, who could easily have been one of his sons.

Shaz came round each Sunday to gain guidance for his 'A' level Literature exam. He called in first to the Home for a guitar lesson with Joseph before arriving at my room. Joseph would tag along now and again to listen to us analysing Conrad's *Heart of Darkness*. The two of them sat on the bed and I, the professor, took the chair. I would select key passages from the text, read them aloud and dissect them in terms of theme and imagery, as I had been taught to do by our English teacher. I had great skill not only in spotting an important image, but in connecting it up with other images in the text. Shaz was full of admiration, though it was really a simple task once you discovered the trick of it. The Congo river coiled like a snake, for instance, was an animal image. Animal images as a general rule betokened moral ugliness, indecency and the like. I drew Shaz's attention to about six other images in the novel to prove the point. Conrad had placed them at strategic points to create a mood of disgust. Reference to birds and fish on the other hand tended to betoken gentleness, spirituality, freedom. By counting the number of animal images against those of fish or bird, it was easy to pinpoint that the work tended towards conveying a sense of horror, or relief from horror. Since there were only, at a stretch, about two fish/bird allusions in the text as opposed to two dozen clear animal ones, it was obvious how Conrad felt about life in the Congo. There was also another standard trick, that of 'the theme of appearance and reality'. All great works of art had this theme thing – the whole of Shakespeare was about what you think you see and what you actually see. In fact, the surest way of identifying what was a work of art from what was just popular literature was to keep a sharp eye out for the theme of appearance and reality. Once you spotted it, you knew you were on the right track.

Joseph, however, was not as impressed as Shaz by my critical skills, and would not hesitate to interrupt with his own interpretation of things. Once, when I was explaining to Shaz the difference between pentameter and trochee in poetry, drumming various rhythms with my fingers on the table, Joseph broke in by stating that it was all foolishness. 'Poetry is like bird,' he said, 'and it gliding or lifting and plunging, wings outspread or beating and curving, and the whole music is in the birdwing.'

'Birdshit!' Shaz retorted on my behalf, convinced of my superior book knowledge of Form.

Joseph was equally adamant. 'What you doing with your pentating and strokee and all dem rules is putting iron-bar one by one in a spacious room so the bird flying round and round and breaking beak and wing against the wall trying to reach the sunlight. You turning all the room in the universe and in the human mind into bird cage.'

'But what you know about poetry?' Shaz challenged him, 'and you can't even write your own name!'

'I don't need to write it,' Joseph said fiercely, 'I know the sound of it,' and as if to prove the point, he strummed his guitar. I continued to drum pentameter and trochee on the table whilst Joseph retaliated by composing a tune around the rhythms, so that after five minutes or so of experimentation the two of us arrived at a harmony like tabla and sitar players.

'At this rate I'll fail all my fucking exams,' Shaz scowled, gathering up his books to go.

Mr Ali, provoked by the noise, came into the room and stared at us. 'What you boys doing,' he demanded, looking around to make sure all the furniture was still there. He rubbed his finger along the windowsill and held up the dirt. 'Room need cleaning, soapwater, cloth, wipe skirting board, window ledge . . . I raise rent, I give notice.' He spoke to Shaz in Urdu telling him how much time and money he had spent on decorating the house and how I must spend a few hours every Sunday wiping the paintwork and scrubbing the sink. 'What in this book?' he asked, picking one out from the pile and flicking through.

'*The Canterbury Tales* Mr Ali,' I replied, anxious to make a good impression so as to secure my tenancy.

He looked closely at a page. 'What in it?' he wanted to know.

'Old-time English, like how they used to write it five-hundred years ago,' I explained. 'It's about a group of religious people going on a pilgrimage to a holy shrine like Muslims going to Mecca.' I mentioned the last bit as a way of eliciting his sympathy, for on my first day he had warned me about cooking pork sausages in the house. It worked, for he was immediately distracted from his concern for cleanliness and did not notice the milk bottle beside the bin, its contents green with fungus. I pounced upon his interest, not giving him time to recover, by rattling on about Chaucer, who wrote in the fourteenth century about all the great concerns of our times, but especially about love for God and fellow human beings. I took the book from him and read aloud, in what I imagined to be the Middle English, a passage from the Prologue. 'You can tell from such a piece what a devout man Chaucer was,' I said, giving him back the book, 'what a fervent believer in God.'

'True,' muttered Mr Ali, taking my word for it. He looked at the book cover and read slowly, '*Canterbury Tales*,' as if resolving to buy a copy on the very next occasion he found himself in a bookshop. 'I got relatives in Canterbury,' he said, 'cousin own grocery. He settled there from Kenya ten years now. Sell fruit and veg. Good business, make much money.' He put down the book and made for the door, sadly, as if talking of his cousin's success had suddenly reminded him of his own relative poverty and failure to live up to immigrant expectations. At his age all he had was a house full of destitute tenants. He was running no business of his own. He did not even have a job. He lived with his wife in two rooms. He mumbled goodbye to Shaz and Joseph and left.

'But what 'bout the way he talk 'bout black people?' Joseph persisted, jumping up from the bed and pacing the room in a sudden agitation.

'What black people?' I asked uncertainly.

He snatched *Heart of Darkness* from my hand and peered at the page, unable to decipher the words, unable to identify the blacks who had obviously set his mind blazing. 'Where the bit about them lying under the trees dying?' he demanded, shoving the book at me.

I flicked through, found the passage and read it aloud to him. 'That's part of the theme of suffering and redemption which lies at the core of the novel's concern,' I stated cogently and intelligently, putting the book down.

'No, it ain't, is about colours. You been saying is a novel 'bout the fall of man, but is really 'bout a dream. Beneath the surface is the dream. The white light of England and the Thames is the white sun over the Congo that can't mix with the green of the bush and the black skin of the people. All the colours struggling to curve against each other like rainbow, but instead the white light want to blot out the black and the green and reduce the world to one blinding colour.'

I was spellbound not so much by his crazy exegesis as by the passion of his outburst, the sudden surge of eloquence. Shaz remained bored, picked up the guitar and strummed idly. Joseph sat on the bed, still agitated, but his voice lowered in confession. 'When you smoke ganja and close your eyes you see dribbles of a thousand lights. And you can't turn them into words because if you speak you wake up and the sunlight wipe out all the little tribes of colours in one rulership. The white man want clear everything away, clear away the green bush and the blacks and turn the whole place into ivory which you can't plant or smoke or eat. Ivory is the heart of the white man,' he concluded professorially.

From then on he seemed to know a new mission in life, for instead of sitting at the window all day staring at the traffic and playing his guitar, he became a regular visitor to my room, pestering me to read aloud passages of Conrad and asking convoluted questions which my training in theme-and-imagery spotting didn't equip me to answer fully. They were daft questions, like what was the colour of the Congo water, what colour was the ivory when it was dug out of the burial ground, do steam ships grow black all over because of the soot, why was the old white woman in the Company's office wearing a white bonnet and knitting black wool, what colour were elephants from which they got white ivory, why did the dying black man have a piece of white thread around his neck, did I think that the green parasol of the chief accountant was like the green of the jungle, and why was the Russian trader dressed like a harlequin, in clothing patched in blue and red and yellow and scarlet and brown? This last question was intriguing. Why indeed had Conrad suddenly introduced a kaleidoscopic burst of colour in the novel, after a narrative of black, white and green? I began to glimpse some sense in Joseph's enquiries and for the first time I turned to him with a question, dropping all the pretence of being the teacher.

'Why does the Russian wear so many colours?' I asked.

'I think,' Joseph replied after some deliberation, 'that

Conrad talking about the theme of appearance and reality.' I considered myself an expert on this particular literary convention and Joseph's appropriation of it left me completely perplexed.

'Look at me,' Joseph continued, 'what colour I am?'

'Black?' I offered, for the first time unsure of what seemed an obvious answer.

'Hmmm,' he replied, deep in thought, 'right, you right, I black, no doubt about it, yes?'

'Yes,' I agreed, caught in uncertainty, looking him up and down to make sure, 'what's the problem?'

'Nothing,' he mumbled, 'it's just that sometimes I wake up middle of night to drink water and when I catch sight in the mirror, is nothing I see. Just blank mirror. And when I look again making a special effort, a black blob of face appear. Like a lump of coal. But how yellow and orange flame can come out of coal? And the coal turn white when it burn out to ash? How come I turn all different colours if you set light to me? And you know what you get when you break down the coal piece by piece until you get to the smallest piece and then you break that?'

I could not guess his riddle.

'Atoms,' he said triumphantly, 'billions and trillions of atoms, each of them smaller than the smallest dot, and you can't touch them or see them. Atoms is like nothing. No taste, no smell, and no colour. Just like air.'

And out of all this banal introspection he emerged with a glimmer of ideas which made me reach for my notepad.

'And don't you think,' he said, 'that when Marlow say nothing about Kurtz in the end, is because nothing left to say, because Kurtz become nothing? He become a word, just a sound, just the name "Kurtz", like the colour "black"? Conrad break he down to what he is, atoms, nothing, a dream, a rumour, a black man. I know what Kurtz is. When I was in borstal I was rumour. They look at me and see ape, trouble, fist. And all the time I nothing, I sleep and wake and eat like zombie, time passing but no sense of time, nothing to look out of the window at, nothing to look in at, and no ideas in my mind, no ideas about where I come from and where I should be going. You can't even see yourself, even if you stand in front of mirror, all you seeing is shape. But all the time they seeing you as animal, riot, nigger, but you know you is nothing, atoms, only image and legend in their minds. So to make yourself real you collect things, and you place them round your room like ritual, like black magic. Your comb always on the table, the teeth facing the door, not the other way around. Your packet of cigarettes and box of matches under your pillow, nowhere else, facing upwards so that you can see the label. Your towel fold in four hanging on the bed-head. Your shoes under the bed, the lace done up and fold in a bow, because you not going nowhere . . . and one day the warden come in looking for drugs or knives or something, and throw everything all about the place, and you know that all your effort to be real is unreal, that you is nothing. But you still try, you fool yourself, and when the warden gone you arrange everything back in their place, collect every matchstick and put them one by one back into the box. What is more strange sometimes is when everything in order and you feeling contented, you will suddenly mess up everything yourself, as if you playing warden. You shake the box of matches all over the floor and kick them in all corners of the room. Then you will go hunting for them, until you have each and every one of them back neatly in the box and under the pillow.'

We continued our meandering, probably meaningless conversation on Conrad for several weeks, Joseph always having something curious to contribute, weaving his personal history into the text, and Shaz's interest steadily waning due to these interventions.

'It's only a daft book you know,' Shaz would say when Joseph took off along some enigmatic flight path of ideas. Once, when Joseph was interrogating us persistently on why Conrad had named Marlow Marlow and Kurtz Kurtz, Shaz told him mockingly that 'Mar' was an anagram of 'ram' and 'low' of 'owl'. Marlow was a ram in that he was persistent like a battering ram, always working, always repairing the boat, always pushing ahead; and like an owl because he refused to dream, in the way that Kurtz was a dreamer, since owls were awake all night when the rest of the world was in fantastic slumber. As to Kurtz, well he was a cur, a human beast; the 'tz' was added to give him a German sounding name, making him out to be the first Nazi. But the crucial thing about the name Kurtz was that it ended in 'z', for he was a boring ass, his story was enough to put anyone to sleep . . . zzzzzzz . . . so we can forget all about Kurtzzzzzz. On the other hand, he is a very puzzzzzling character. The 'z' was also zero which was what Kurtz turned black people into, and himself, in his deeds of extermination.

Joseph was unperturbed by this nonsense. He told us about Jack Askey, one of the wardens in the Borstal. The 'key' part was obvious, since he locked them up at night. And he was a Jack/as(s) because in the daytime he brayed at them or aimed vicious kicks when they showed surliness at his commands. When he thought no one was looking he would enter the cell of his favourite boy and mount him donkey-fashion. 'Words are so full of cleverness,' Joseph said, 'I wish I could learn how to read and write them. Every word is cat with nine separate lives, it come up to you for tickling and stroking and feeding, or it wander away and walk along neighbour's garden fence, or it crouch and concentrate when it see bird or it fall asleep under the bonnet of nearest parked car.'

'That's silly,' Shaz retaliated, 'words are just a bunch of letters we form to identify things. How many lives the word "and" have for example?'

Joseph took up the challenge: without 'and' the whole sentence would collapse like one of those high-rise blocks of flats in Stockwell. 'And' was the steel girder holding up the flesh of concrete. 'And' was like the pylon supporting electricity cables. 'And' was like Marlow's rivets he was always crying out for that made the boat hold together.

He would have continued this endless tossing out of images, until Shaz flung the Conrad at him in a gesture of frustration and surrender. 'Why you're so poor and will never get anywhere with your life and always scrounge off the dole is because you're thick. You're full of shitty useless dreamy ideas. You'll never work for a living because you too doped up with unreal thoughts.'

And that was nearly the end of the relationship between Shaz and Joseph. From then on, for two months or so, he lost the privilege of guitar lessons from Joseph and was stuck in the same unmanageable chord whenever he came to visit. 'That boy is a real donkey,' Shaz said, 'a real arsehole.'

Joseph turned up one Sunday afternoon wearing a raincoat with a huge bulge. It was a fiery afternoon, one of those rare English summer days when the sky actually blasted down showers of heat instead of the normal sickly dribble of rain. He was sweating heavily. He must have been a spectacle on the road, wrapped in a raincoat when all about people were cavorting half-stripped in parks and ice-cream vans were kerb-crawling for mothers and infants. No one though took much notice of him, accustomed as they were to the sight of black youth wearing colourful drapes over their heads beneath which snaked locks of hair, or fetching heavy radio-cassette players on their shoulders like Caliban's logs. It was impolite to stare, and in any case they were dangerous creatures, quick to take offence, whip out knives or claw at people's faces. You merely giggled or fumed behind their backs and wished that they would be banished back to the trees of Africa and the West Indies. It was indecent the way young daughters nurtured for fifteen years through school and home abandoned love and sense to fondle their tails in dance halls.

Joseph was just another strange nigger with a hump under his raincoat when he entered my room and announced that he had stolen it. I was busy in a book which I put aside reluctantly to give him my attention. He unbuttoned the raincoat and drew out a cardboard box. I watched impassively as he undid the string, wishing he would disappear so that I could continue working. He pulled out a black contraption resembling a camera and put it on the table before me like a tribute.

'What is it?' I asked, suppressing my excitement at the solid, expensive-looking gadget arrayed with dials and switches.

'A different kind of book,' he said, delighted by the thing, 'a real video-cassette camera,' and he touched it to make sure it was not a mirage. A drop of sweat ran from the tip of his finger and trickled along a groove in the plastic.

'You'll pay for this you know,' I told him, my voice suddenly assuming an ominous tone.

When Shaz resumed his visits, Joseph set up his camera, adjusted our seating so that we were facing each other by the window to take full advantage of the light, pinned microphones to our collars, hiding the wires beneath our jumpers, took voice-control samples and, after elaborate preparations and false starts (from

Joseph forgetting to plug in the machine to discovering he had left the sound switch off), we launched our discussion at the shout of 'Take one'; Shaz's first duty being to hold up a piece of cardboard with the number '1' drawn on it. When he put the cardboard away, we began properly, analysing passages in Conrad's novel. Shaz, the camera focused on him, made strenuous efforts at eloquence, struggling to say things that were intelligent and impressive. He kept staring at the camera when it was my turn to speak so that it was difficult to maintain a thread of discussion between us. At one session he came along well prepared, having read a book of criticism and learned by heart some impressive phrases which he rehearsed to the camera. Unfortunately it was on one of those frequent occasions when Joseph had pressed the wrong combination of switches so that nothing was recorded on the tape. Shaz broke out in indecent expressions, accusing him of primitive incompetence. 'You're just like one of those savages chewing bones on the river bank and scooting off whenever the white man blows the steamer-horn.' As if to prove the point about Joseph's incomprehension of white man's technology, he picked up the book, found the passage about the African fireman and read it triumphantly aloud to the camera, telling Joseph to roll the film.

Joseph was unmoved, merely studied the dials of his camera, turning on a switch here and there, trying out various combinations. Shaz became more and more agitated, finally exploding in an outburst about the stupidity of niggers and how unscientific they were.

'You're like a monkey playing with all those dials, and you don't have a clue what they mean. The white man has got to regret the day he took you people out of the bush and showed you science. After three hundred years you still can't figure out how the magic works.' But Joseph was deeply involved in plugging and unplugging wires and didn't seem to hear. He fished out a knife from his back pocket, peeled the end off a wire, bit it, placed a plastic tube over it and slotted it back into a crevice in the camera.

'I can't read nor write but I can see,' he said, after Shaz had gone, his attention still focused on wires and switches, 'and that is what this camera for.' I watched him quietly, wanting to apologise for Shaz's crudeness but not knowing what to say. He was, after all, genuinely incompetent, always having problems with getting the camera to operate properly in spite of his great enthusiasm. He was full of unrealistic half-formed ideas which he didn't have the resources to develop. Everything was contained in books and he was handicapped by illiteracy.

When he returned later in the week, he was obsessed with Africa, but I could not help him, being ignorant myself of that subject. 'But you read books,' he argued, 'it must all be in one book somewhere.' I tried to explain that there were millions of books, and I had to concentrate on a small number for my 'A' levels. In ten years or so I'd know more about everything. But he could not wait, urging me to find a book on Africa which told the whole story.

'Is true what Shaz say about black people, that we

don't have any chemistry and sums and all that?'

I told him not to bother with Shaz, he was only being wilful and vicious.

'But is true or a lie? That we walk about naked with other people's bones through our noses? That we eat each other?'

None of us had any answers to these questions. The only pictures of Africa were those on television, mostly waterless children, flies, deserts. We collected stamps and milk tops at school and posted them off to charities. Classes vied with each other to collect the greatest number of sackfuls and when the letters of thanks arrived from Oxfam or Christian Aid, our teacher pinned them on the noticeboard for all to see.

'I am going to make a film on the Conrad,' Joseph announced at one of our study sessions.

Shaz laughed.

'How?' I asked, humouring him.

'You will need a cast of hundreds and costumes, never mind the river and a lot of jungle,' Shaz scoffed.

Joseph said nothing, his mind enraptured by the idea of a film.

'And what about the steamship, how would you manage that?' Shaz mocked.

'There's always a way,' Joseph said quietly, 'all you have to do is think about it. Everything in the world is there for us to take, we only have to do so.'

'It's not "take" you mean, but "thieve",' Shaz said, 'because if you don't earn something you can only thieve it. You think people will just come up to you and say "here Mr Joseph, film-maker, please have this steamship as a present? Please have this camera and a thousand cassettes?" '

'Nobody own the tree and the water, and nobody can stop you looking at a ship moor on a river,' he said, 'or at moonlight. I going to put everything together in pretend form so when you look at the film you will think is Africa.'

He invited me to be his producer, and every afternoon after school I met him at Tooting Bec Common which was to be the location of his film. It had everything, trees, pond and clumps of bush with which to re-create a feel of the African landscape. He stood under a large tree and pointed the camera, scanning the branches, zooming closer to capture a sense of dense foliage blacking out the sky. He threw stones in the pond to create a movement in the water, which would pass for the trail of a river boat. He lay flat on his stomach and inched towards a patch of tall grass, the snout of his camera pushing through the blades, suggesting a hazardous journey through the jungle. Some small boys stopped their ballplay and wandered over, curious. 'It's a film we are making,' I said solemnly as I watched Joseph's posterior disappearing in the grass.

They stood in awe. 'You from the television?' one asked, staring at me hard as if recognising my face from the screen, perhaps one of the black pop singers.

'Can I have your autograph mister?' another asked shyly.

I didn't have any writing paper in my bag, only a few text books, so he held out his hand and I signed 'Jackson Stardust' in his palm because it sounded like an appropriate name for a celebrity. He looked at me in wonderment, turned and broke into a trot homewards, his fist clenched as if to prevent the signature from escaping. Whilst Joseph was cavorting in the grass I signed half a dozen tiny palms, and all the white plastic squares on the ball. After this experience of fame I had no hesitation in following Joseph on his various locations, for we always attracted a small crowd, or at least curious stares from passers-by. Two months had elapsed since he had stolen the camera, and the familiarity of ownership lowered his defences. He no longer took the camera on the bus wrapped in a Sainsbury's plastic bag. It lay openly on his lap for all to see. It was only when a policeman sauntered up to us as Joseph was filming a restaurant boat anchored by Westminster Bridge that he resumed a little caution. We told the officer that we were doing a school project on landmarks in London. He looked hard at the expensive camera and then at Joseph in his shabby jeans and raincoat. He looked at me in my school blazer and grey trousers. 'We are doing Big Ben afterwards, then Nelson's Column, then 10 Downing Street, then we are going back to Balham,' I blurted out nervously. Joseph was totally calm, smiling cordially at the officer. He was accustomed to dealing with them. He knew how to conciliate them with a silly nigger grin.

He came with us to Battersea Fun Fair soon after we started, for when I told him about the World Cruise he immediately recognised the ideal film setting. The painted scenes of Africa were exactly suited to his purposes and he spent many early-morning hours filming them from all angles, doing close-ups, and all manner of other tricks, before hordes of pleasure-seekers descended upon him, interrupting his studies. It was doubtful whether any image was captured on the tape at all, given the darkness of the World Cruise, and he had no way of telling, not having the opportunity yet of stealing a machine to play the tape. Nevertheless he took up his position every morning for a whole week, leaning precariously from the boat and pointing his camera to the pictures. He came out once soaked and nearly vomiting, having fallen in and swallowed a mouthful of oily water. He was covered in a film of oil which had been leaking from the engine room for some time now. Shaz and I rushed over to him, but he was not in the least concerned, for the camera was safe and dry. We took some money illegally from the till and told him to take a taxi home, having to argue loudly with him for he was insisting on continuing his filming.

'He's a bit crazy but I like him a lot,' Shaz confessed as we were waiting for the bus home one night, 'all this filming has become an obsession with him.' It had been a good day's work with four hours overtime and fifteen shillings defrauded from the proprietors. 'We will have to be careful he doesn't get us the sack though,' Shaz continued. He was right. Mr King was an extremely stern manager and would have dismissed us on the spot if he discovered that we had given Joseph the freedom of his World Cruise. Also, Joseph had become discontented with some of the African pictures, had brought his own paint brush and tampered with the landscape, to fulfil the demands of his filming. He painted over some figures, added others; he re-arranged the wildlife. A white man sucking on a bone and firing a gun pointlessly in the air took his place among the native savages. I think he must have been Mr Kurtz. There was also a dead elephant lying on its back, four massive feet stuck in the air like the chimney stacks of Battersea power station which lay just outside the Fun Fair and which provided the model for Joseph's artistry. Two white men, small like pygmies against the massive body of the dead animal, had climbed upon its head and were tugging at its ivory tusks, as if to pull them out. Mr King would not have liked all these unofficial changes to the Congo even though Joseph's work was meticulous and a definite improvement upon the original artist's work. 'It's good the way he can turn his hand to anything,' Shaz continued, 'whether guitar playing or painting. He's got real talent.'

I nodded, not being in a communicative mood, anxious to get home to finish off some reading. But Shaz was joyful tonight and wanted to talk because he had met a girl who fancied him. 'I like the funfair you know,' he said with real pleasure in his voice. 'I wouldn't mind giving up school and working here full-time, what do you think?'

'It's so so,' I replied, thinking of what a doom it would be to have to spend the rest of my life in the funfair. There was surface glamour and excitement, certainly.

During my lunch-break I would wander from stall to stall, throwing the odd rings to win a prize, firing the gun, staying to play a game of bingo or jumping on the roller-coaster and wallowing in terror as we rode and pitched and swung at the very edge of the ride, the car threatening to plunge off the rails and fall fifty feet to earth, and all of us, strangers, screaming in a fellowship of panic and pleasure. But mostly I sat on a boat and read a book quietly, wanting to belong to the crowd, but knowing I had to do something serious with my life, or else I might as well die.

'What's the matter,' Shaz would ask, 'let's go and have some fun. Pick up some birds or something.'

'I can't afford to,' I would say, 'you go, I have to finish a couple of chapters.'

He went off silently.

Like Joseph I wanted to be somebody and the only way to achieve this was to acquire a collection of good examination results and go to university. Everything was planned: I would try for top grades in my three 'A' levels, then I'd do a B.A. Degree at Oxford or Cambridge and then a Ph.D. I would write books, and one day become a celebrity, or writer, or something. I was seventeen now, and nobody, but in ten years time I'd be a somebody.

'It will take twenty years of hard work and studying; why don't you just do a few exams and get a job with lots of money?' Shaz wanted to know.

'Because that is the way I am,' I told him, mysteriously, 'money's not everything,' and as soon as I spoke the words the memory of a drunken Richilo sliding about in the mud, like a new calf unsteady on its legs, returned. I put down the book, wondering what had become of him, of my grandparents, of Albion Village. It had been a long time since I had heard by letter from my mother. The last one told how the girls growing up and doing well. The eldest secure job as typist, the rest still taking schooling. Things be in short supply. People have to queue up all day for flour. Auntie Pakul supplying them with vegetables and rice. Two of Pa's cows impounded. They wander into someone garden and munch up all the plants. He did have to pay 100 dollars to release them. Matam's wife die of sugar-in-the-blood, one huge funeral hold, and the rum shop close up for a day. 'Zulu' showing at the Globe Cinema, and the place pack out with niggers. The house need repairing but wood so expensive it have to wait for a year.

Whenever I wrote back I always told her that I was eating and reading a lot because that would please her. I have a summer job earning a good salary (I always translated the £10 a week into Guyana dollars for it sounded like an enormous sum then), and I enclose twenty dollars for you. The shops in England are crammed with goods, anything anybody could wish for. The English are very nice to us. I have my own apartment and because I am doing so brilliantly at school the Government has decided to pay the rent and give me an allowance (this sounded much more comforting than being in care). I will come home after my 'A' levels before I go to University to study law or medicine. I have been commissioned to advise on a children's script for BBC television and at this very moment Mr Joseph, a leading young director, is doing the preliminary filming. It will be like 'Zulu', set in Africa, lots of excitement and action, and Mr Joseph is thinking of inviting Michael Caine to take the leading part, since he is now married to that beautiful Guyanese woman. I'm bound to meet them during the filming and will get an autograph for the girls.

I caught my reflection in the water, waving, mocking. Another face appeared, and I looked up to see Janet. 'Dreaming again,' she laughed gently.

I mumbled something.

Monica, her companion, Shaz's girlfriend, came up. 'We want a ride,' she demanded, looking at me with a wicked light in her eyes.

'Sure,' I said, and they climbed in the boat and glided away. I went to meet them at the other end. Janet stumbled as she climbed out and I thrust my hand out to support her. It slipped from her shoulder and clutched her breast. Monica giggled and walked away to meet Shaz who had just returned from his lunch-break and was re-positioning himself in his ticket office. I fumbled with the boats whilst Janet leaned against the railings watching me.

'Can I have another ride?' she asked sweetly.

I looked up to see her smiling, waiting for an answer. 'Sure,' and I pointed her to the boat at the front of the queue.

She walked over and sat down, re-arranging her skirt, waiting for me to untie the rope and set her free. I walked towards her, hesitating as I heard Monica break out into a cackle as Shaz said something to her.

'Come and ride with me,' Janet said. I imagined I could sense the trembling of her voice. She looked at me as I leaned to push the boat off. 'Come in then,' she urged. I hesitated, 'Come in,' she repeated. I stepped into the boat and we glided away to the sound of raucous laughter. 'She's a right slut,' Janet said, after a few minutes of embarrassed silence. In the darkness her voice was startling clear. She spoke with a lilting country accent.

'Where do you come from?' I ventured.

'Kent, a place just outside Maidstone, on the coast.'

That explained the music in her speech. 'What are you doing down here?' I continued, as the boat manoeuvred the first corner, bumping and grating the concrete bend. In the light reflected from the paintings, I could see her hand resting on the lip of the boat. 'Careful,' I said, 'or you'll injure your fingers.' I reached automatically for her hand to place it inside the boat. She laughed softly, embarrassed by my touch. 'It's beautiful in here, isn't it?' I resumed for want of something more meaningful to say.

'Mmmm, a bit spooky and mysterious.'

We passed some African country crowded with naked men and women planting yams and I lowered my eyes in shame, wishing Joseph had had the opportunity to refashion the place with more civilised images of oil wells, libraries and airports. 'My mum and dad moved to Wimbledon; he's an engineer,' she said, answering my earlier question. I told her I lived in Balham and she was excited since it was not far from her. She asked whether she could come around and I told her my address. We settled on a Wednesday. She played hockey then at a local girls' club which she hated, so she would feign illness or forge a note from her parents saying she was wanted home early so that she could come and see me.

'Nice looking piece, your Janet,' Shaz commented, as we waited for the bus. 'She's got bedroom eyes and a lovely face and big tits, a right baby doll. Monica's a bit stringy, nowhere to put your mouth, nothing to fasten on to.' He burst out laughing. I said nothing, secretly hurt that he should speak of Janet in such a vulgar, open way.

'Have you done it yet?' he asked, an eager gleam in his eyes.

'Done what?' I replied in a faraway voice, pretending to be tired after the long day's work and craning forward to see if a bus was on its way. We were in the middle of a queue and I didn't want anyone to overhear our conversation.

'You know what . . .' he answered, a grin on his face.

'No . . . it's too early,' I said shyly, overcome by a sense of inadequacy. I knew that Shaz was more advanced in these matters. After a mere day's acquaintance with Monica he had already taken her for several rides in the World Cruise and had recounted in vivid, hungry detail how he had raised her jumper and moved his tongue along her chest, nibbling at her armpits, biting her neck, slipping his hand down her unzipped jeans. Although I had read about all these adult things in books of fiction I had no idea how they were to be done, but I maintained a certain dignity with Shaz, refusing to seek his advice. Even when he turned up one morning with a girlie magazine and sat in the boat gaping at the pictures, I pretended to be apathetic, merely glancing over his shoulders now and again as he shoved a nude at me for comment, and carrying on with my work of sweeping the concrete.

'Here,' he said, giving the magazine to me when the time came for him to open the ticket booth, 'gaze on these dolls and dream.'

'You keep it,' I said primly, 'I've got to re-read bits of this book today. I'll look at it tomorrow.'

'You're just like that Marlow,' he said, in a flash of intelligence, 'all work and no play. "Rivets are no substitute for a pair of tits; discuss with reference to . . ."' That would make a good exam question, eh? I'd get a distinction, boy!' He walked away laughing, triumphantly.

Janet had come on Wednesday afternoon as promised. I had taken the whole day off work just to tidy my room, scrub the skirting board, put a new plastic liner in the bin, wipe the windows and, in an act of desperate desire, change the sheets on my bed. Mr Ali, disturbed by the commotion, knocked and entered just as I was dipping a sponge in a bucket of soapy water to wipe the floor. It was a happy intervention for he had been pestering me for weeks to keep the room clean and even threatening me with notice to leave. I was beginning to hate him. The room was generally untidy, the bed unmade, books scattered everywhere, and the usual pile of greasy, unwashed cups and plates in the sink. I kept my dirty laundry in an old suitcase under the bed out of sight, and would venture out to the machines at the top of the road only when I had run out of clean clothing. For an Asian, though, he seemed to have no respect for education. He should have known my circumstances, not having parents and all that, and been more sympathetic, I argued to myself, after all books are more worthy than hygiene. It was in this precious, superior frame of mind that I would listen to him haranguing me for being untidy, not taking in anything because I was secure in the knowledge of great literature.

By the time Janet arrived, not only had I completely transformed the room but I had spent my last few shillings on an expensive cake and three varieties of tea biscuits which were proudly displayed on the table. It was two days before the next Social Security cheque arrived, or the weekly wage from the Fun Fair, but I didn't care, I would either steal supplies from the Asian corner shop or else live on the remains of the cake and tea biscuits. My sense of poverty took on a certain aura of romance.

She looked around the room as I fiddled with the kettle, wondering whether I should have attempted to kiss her on the cheek as soon as she had entered.

It was too late now. She was sitting on the bed, a full minute had elapsed, it would hardly be proper to kiss her now. On what pretext? Perhaps when she was about to leave I could try; after all, it was natural to do so at that particular time. I turned round to see only her eyes gazing at me and I wished I could just touch her face or run my hand gently over her brown hair hanging in pretty shoulder-length curls. I stirred the coffee, feeling silly at those small desires, thinking how Shaz would have laughed at me for not wanting more.

We talked mostly about books; her parents were wealthy, sending her to a fee-paying school where she was taking History, Literature and Religious Education for 'A' Levels. We compared syllabuses. I wondered whether I was being a bore, but I could think of no other topic of conversation. When she asked me about Guyana my mind went blank. It was somehow impossible to talk about Albion Village, and how as a boy I would set out in the morning with my grandmother to hunt crabs, the two of us scouting behind mounds of mud looking for their colonies; when we discovered them, we scooped them up with a spade into a cloth bag and took them home to be curried. We nibbled politely at the chocolate biscuits and talked instead about London, about our favourite teachers, about the job at Battersea Fun Fair. I wondered secretly why she went about with Monica who appeared to be wholly different in her sloppy manner and unabashed sexuality. She seemed to have read my thoughts, for the conversation switched to Monica.

'She hangs about streets, late at night . . .,' Janet blurted out.

I didn't understand.

'Bedford Hill, she makes a lot of money,' Janet continued shyly.

'You mean with men?' I asked, amazed, 'but she's only sixteen or so, it's against the law!'

Janet blushed and laughed. I sat on the bed, not knowing what more to say, looking down at my shoes, noticing the smudges and the mud stains, realising with a feeling of foolishness that in all the furious hours of tidying up the room I had completely forgotten to clean them. 'I ought to go now,' she said, getting up, smoothing her skirt and waiting for my response.

I shuffled towards the door, opened it, and let her out, wanting to say something significant, to be memorable in these final moments. I wished I were important, somebody, instead of being drowned in a sense of orphaned neglect. I hoped she was suitably impressed by the array of books at least. In re-arranging them on the shelves in preparation for her visit I had rehearsed a little speech. I would talk to her about *Troilus and Criseyde*, 'a great poem in praise of love', as one of our essay titles expressed it. Perhaps she would disagree, we would get into a long conversation about the substance of the romance and I would quote to her the Latin phrase our teacher used in summarising the tragedy of the tale, 'sunt lachrimae rerum' – 'there are tears in things'. I imagined our conversation would pause at this dual moment of poignancy and erudition, that she would be moved by both. As it was, all my expectations were dashed, for the Chaucer her school was doing was the 'Prologue' to *The Canterbury Tales* set by a different examination board from ours. I could have fallen back on the familiar territory of Conrad, which we were both studying, but the sex there, and the description of blacks in the bush, were too shameful for me to contemplate in her company.

'Can I come and see you next week?' she asked as I opened the front door for her.

'Yes,' I replied, eagerly, embarrassed by the suddenness in my voice.

'Good,' she said, kissed me on the cheek and walked away sprightly, not looking back. I was speechless, lingered at the door before wandering upstairs in an idiot daze. I felt great hunger and ate all three packets of tea-biscuits. I went to bed feeling sick.

'We kissed . . .,' I answered Shaz as he persisted in his questions. He gave a vulgar laugh. Bored with the traffic I glanced up idly to the church steeple adjacent to the pub, curious as to how long ago it was built, perhaps in the last century. There was probably a stone somewhere on the façade with a date inscribed. It was too dark to see now. Nobody goes to the church these days, not even me. I dug my hand into my pocket, touched by guilt, and, feeling the coins, promised to stop stealing. People were flocking into the pub across the road where a band struck up loud electric music. Shaz listened intently to the guitars which to my ear made hideous, uncoordinated noises. I hated pubs. He and I wandered into the same pub a few weeks back, after another late night at the Fun Fair. It was full of smoke and big white men with tattoos on their arms and heavy boots, drinking themselves silly. I remembered Nasim running down the road chased by a horde of drunks and louts, and lingered by the doorway, hiding myself partially behind a pillar. Shaz was more reckless. He strode up to the bar and ordered two half-pints, seemingly unconcerned by all the whites around him who were looking at him strangely.

I wished the bus would come. It was already dark, we would not get home until nine. I had an essay to work on and the next day would be extremely busy since Janet was paying another visit. I would have to get up early, spend the whole morning cleaning up the room and go shopping for food. I had decided that since I could not afford to take her out for a proper meal I would cook something for the two of us. I would make an effort for her. This would certainly involve theft at the local corner-shop. I had managed to lower the Asian's guard over the months by striking up conversations in broken English on the subject of visas and citizenship with which he seemed obsessed. One long discussion in particular focused on the meaning of the word 'indefinite' (he showed me his passport which had stamped on it 'permitted to remain in the United Kingdom for an indefinite period') – did 'indefinite' mean 'forever', 'unlimited', or was it that the Home Office was still processing his application to stay and could send him home any day now, in which case 'indefinite' meant 'undefined'? As soon as he turned his back to the cash register to give change to a customer I would secrete a jar of marmite or tin of sardines, remembering with gratitude Pocket Patel and his patient tuition. He would have been pleased by my deft action. If a particular shoplifting venture was successful, I would be generous in turn, reassuring the Asian that 'indefinite' – in the oldest, or strictest, or commonest sense of the word – meant he could remain here as long as he wanted. If, however, circumstances prevented me leaving the shop with a good haul I would terrify him by talking about the difference between 'traditional usage' and 'modern legal usage', the latter possibly meaning that 'indefinite' could be interpreted as 'yet to be decided'. The Home Office was full of Oxford- and Cambridge-educated lawyers, so anything was possible from these clever men. He would grow dismal, muttering about how English was so hard, how every word had a dozen different understandings, how he could barely pronounce the words, never mind glean their multiple meanings. I felt sorry for him, but I needed to keep him on edge so as to sustain his need to converse with me. I consoled myself with the thought that the English language was not of my personal making, and that I could not be held responsible for the way it bewildered and hurt people.

The traffic weaved in and out of streets, as confused and meandering as my thoughts. Still no bus came.

I rehearsed in my mind how I would greet Janet tomorrow, what stories I would tell her of the past week's adventures at the Fun Fair. My deepest wish was to move her to extreme emotion, to create laughter and sadness. It was obvious that I could not impress her with money, a privileged background, sartorial elegance, dancing skills or sheer handsomeness. All I had at my disposal was the gift of stories, the alien experiences of which would possibly seduce her, given her intelligent and enquiring nature. I wondered whether she would seriously incline to certain exotic recollections of Guyana, and resolved to try out on her the story of Gladys's devotion to the goddess Kali which suddenly disturbed my mind and which seemed so ridiculous and misplaced in the setting of traffic, bricks, whites. Gladys, a black woman, and her small girl-child were close to malnutrition. My mother had sent me to the shop to buy some bread for them. She led me into the kitchen where I deposited the bread. The child was asleep on the floor, half-wrapped in a rice-bag. Her face was covered in sores which attracted flies. The house was bare. There were two empty cardboard boxes, some clothing hung from nails in the wall and a thick wooden bench which from its ornate polished handles was obviously a cast-off from a church. At first I did not notice the cock, the kitchen being the darkest room in the house, having only one wooden shutter which she had unexpectedly padlocked. It was only when I felt something soft brush my foot that I saw the hapless bundle.

'What is it Gladys?' I shouted, jumping back.

'Fowlcock, what else it look like?' she answered sadly.

The cock was trussed up in her kitchen, a black string wound around its feet, then around its neck and beak. A piece of red rag protruded from its anus. Some of its feathers had been removed, so that patches of skin were exposed. It made faint movements, the life within it numbed by an unknown terror. I strained to remember all the details, the pot of boiling water, the bunch of feathers nailed to the wall beneath a picture of Kali, like a rough bouquet, and Gladys's face swollen with grief and expectation.

'Is true – true black people doing Indian magic nowadays,' my mother exclaimed when I described the scene of cock, coloured string, picture of Indian goddess on the wall and feather bouquet, 'belly wind blow down all prejudice and people going crazy with need.' And there was hunger everywhere, strikes, riots, bombs exploding late at night and people hiding in their houses as soon as darkness fell, with an arsenal of knives, cutlasses, sticks. For weeks my mother gathered us together in her room as soon as we arrived home from school, and padlocked the door. We could not go out to play. We sat on our bed practising sums on our slates or else the girls helped her sew torn clothing. She produced food from a large basin under the bed when it was time to eat. My sisters had to use a posy since my mother would not open the door to allow them to use the toilet. She allowed me to pee out of the window. We all had to speak in whispers. She drew the blinds and turned on an oil lamp to its dimmest position. It was exciting to begin with, as we all hid under the sheets, jostling each other for a larger space on her bed. She slept on a chair by the door, a pair of scissors close at hand.

None of us knew why the black people and Indian people were killing each other, and who was doing the murdering. Everything was normal at school between all the children. We all queued up excitedly every lunchtime with our enamel bowls when the church van arrived with massive pots of food. The priests and white people in smart uniforms smiled as they piled our plates high with cook-up rice and fried plantains. Each of us was given a Pepsi, or lemonade or milk. Every day was like a party, with lots of nice free food and drinks. It was as if we were special children and the white people had come from far away to give us a treat.

'Why white people giving we so much food?' I asked my mother one night as we hid under the sheets.

'Because they good, kind people, not nasty and stupid like we colonial trash. Is great curse will come on this country if the white people pack up and go.'

She would get up at nine and turn on the radio to catch the news of the fighting. It was taking place far away, in Georgetown. The black people were beating up Indians, burning down their shops and houses. The Indians were fleeing to the countryside.

'Trouble bound to come this way,' my mother muttered in distress, clutching her breast, 'we had better pack up soon and go down Albion Village.'

'Who creating the trouble, and why they fighting?' I asked again.

'Don't ask stupidness,' she said, too upset at the

thought of uprooting us to the safety of our grand-mother's to bother with an explanation, 'just all of you close your eyes and sleep till morning.'

It was my big sister who discovered the reason for the violence. I don't know how she found out and she would not tell us, just so as to feel superior to the rest of us. I guessed she saw it in a newspaper because she was the only one among us who could read one from top to bottom and page to page. As I scratched about on my slate I would watch her reading quietly to herself, feeling proud of her and wishing I could grow up quickly so that I too could understand the words in her book.

'The people fighting for Independence and killing one another because the Indians want to rule after Independence but the blacks also want to do the rul-ing.'

When we asked her, however, what 'Independence' was, she wasn't sure, so we lapsed into a state of ignorance. When we pressed her, my mother didn't know what 'Independence' was either. All she said was that some black and Indian educated people in Georgetown wanted to kick the white people out, take over the land and set up a Government.

'But how can educated people be so blasted foolish to want to hurt the whites,' she cursed, 'we only go turn the whole place into starvation land. See how we suffering already! How they know how to run Govern-ment? How they know how to own factory and repair machine and cause electricity to run in light-bulb and build car? You ever hear such stupidness?'

'If black people hate we so much,' I asked her, 'why Gladys doing Hindu magic?'

'Ssssh!' my mother replied, 'don't talk so loud, you want people kill we?' There was genuine terror in her eyes. 'Don't ever say that black people and we hate each other or your throat will cut and your sisters rape up like they do in Wismar. If anybody ask you anything,' she addressed us all in a warning tone, 'say we is all one people, all of we is neighbour and mattie.'

I wanted to ask who the people were doing the molestation so I'd know who to look out for, but she turned the lights out and ordered us to fall asleep right away.

The sound of breaking glass broke my dream. A crowd of men and women rushed across the street from the pub. The people at the bus stop scattered, some running, others walking away briskly, glancing back in terror. I didn't know what was happening. Shaz was still there, in front of me. Even before I realised that a fight was taking place, he was grabbing my coat and pulling me to a safe distance. We stood under the church steeple and watched the crowd from the pub break up into small groups of agitated men. Their female companions stood on the pavement screaming or sobbing. The groups were fighting in the middle of the street. The traffic flowed past regardless, the drivers too afraid to stop in case their cars got damaged. A white man was lying on the ground, his head hanging from the lip of the pavement. Two white men stood over him as he struggled to get up. They kicked him in the stomach and he collapsed, vomit pouring from his mouth. He rose again, dazed, one hand trying to cover his face. They waited until he was half-upright before slamming their feet into his guts. This time he fell and lay still. Two of the women ran over to protect him, but the men shoved them back, punching one of them in the face. She pressed her hands to her eyes and screamed as if blinded by the blow. The man on the pavement was obviously unconscious, but they raised up his head by the hair and kicked him in the face. He fell like a dead weight, making no noise, not even a feeble groan. Again they picked him up and kicked his head. Three men from a second group rushed over and set upon the two men. One had a beer bottle in his hand which he smashed against the road. The glass broke in our direction. I was paralysed by terror, utterly calm, seeming to see everything in slow motion. The broken bottle was raised and plunged into someone's back. I could see its edge glinting in the lamplight, radiating particles of glass as it rose and fell and tunnelled into flesh in one prolonged delayed motion, one sensuous curve of hatred.

III

JOSEPH POINTED HIS CAMERA for hours to an empty sky, lying on his back in Tooting Bec Common, careless of people walking their dogs, and the two tramps who at night slept in the public toilets adjoining the tennis courts and in the daytime journeyed from bin to bin. He had lost all curiosity in *things*. He no longer even wanted to steal a video player with which to view the images he was gathering on tape. He explained fitfully to Shaz and I why he had abandoned his Conrad project. By piecing his rambling explanations together it became clear that he had developed an interest in nothingness, colourlessness, the sightlessness of air, wind, the pure space between trees rather than leaves clinging on to branches as if in terror of being blown away, or roots clutching frantically, digging down into the earth.

'Everything living off everything else, parasite, hanging on, begging not to let go. Is like hanging on a tower-block edge, only hand snatch to television aerial preventing you falling. Better to let go, be free, feel body-less, weight-less, be yourself, no dependency, just you and space.'

When I asked him why he was bothering to film what could not be seen, he muttered something about just having to, as if he was doomed by his profession as an artist to seek out what was forever beyond him, to concretise what could not even be thought, or, in his own, less lofty words, 'to trap your breath in a paper bag full of holes, the more you blow, the more it escaping, so you pant and fret and your head growing wild with irritation till you want to smash up the whole fucking world.' Shaz interpreted his new mood privately to me as the curse of the black race. According to him, when blacks can't make it, they give up totally and adopt a religion of being nothing, knowing nothing, doing nothing. They become believers in the after-life, instead of the here and now. They start talking about values and morals, quality instead of quantity. What it meant was hanging around street corners smoking dope or going on protest marches to preserve their dignity instead of going out looking for work. Or else they would riot and burn the place down, using their blackness as the coal to feed flames. Burn, burn, burn, that's all they secretly wanted to do. No wonder Joseph was fascinated by the wind, because it was the wind that spread fires.

As he gave this opinion, I looked at him and saw a youthful version of the Asian shopkeeper seated at the till, dwarfed by the coffee jars, toilet rolls, tins of sardines and other groceries packed high and tightly on his shelves, like insulation and complete protection against the cold world outside the shop door. A world of uncertain citizenship, dole queues, ever-hostile whites and shop-lifting blacks, shabby council flats overrun by pimps and drug addicts. For all his reckless talk of guitar playing and art images, I began to suspect that deep down Shaz was a trader craving to possess things, to buy and sell them, and that Joseph's position was more adventurous, more courageous. Or perhaps it was the reverse: Joseph didn't have the opportunity or ability to own things, so out of desperation and cowardice he settled for nothing, whilst Shaz, really wanting to be artistic, was driven by family and cultural expectations to become a businessman.

Whatever the truth, Joseph's talk of space became real to me when Mr Ali's sister died. She had turned up from Pakistan one afternoon, an old bent woman wrapped in a sari. Mr and Mrs Ali had collected her from Heathrow since she could speak no English and did not know how to travel on the train. She was on a three-month holiday visa but, apart from the final visit to the hospital, never once did she step outside the front door, spending all her days on a makeshift bed of mattress and blankets laid out on the living-room floor, coughing endlessly and shivering from the cold, even when the heating was turned up to sauna strength. I rarely saw her in the daytime, except on those few occasions when I ventured downstairs to give Mr Ali his rent or to pay him ten pence for taking a bath. He normally came to my room to collect his dues regular as clockwork at the end of the week, but the worry of his sister's illness so distracted him that his routine was disturbed for the whole period she stayed with us. His behaviour also changed drastically.

Whenever he came to my room, he no longer scrutinised the wallpaper or floor for evidence of stains and dirt. What used to be quick, hostile visits, ameliorated only by my handing over the rent, became leisurely affairs: Mr Ali, face drawn, eyes softened with grief, sitting on my bed talking endlessly about his family. The thickness of his accent and his frequent lapses into Urdu meant it was difficult to follow him, but I was a model of patience, listening intently, nodding sympathetically, breaking out with the odd apostrophe as if his suffering was also mine. Although largely bored by his stories, I affected an interest since it put him under an obligation to me. For the first time I had some control over him, so that I could negotiate late payment of the rent because I had spent some of it on food or a book that week.

His sister, apparently, had been sick for a year; no one knew why. A widow, she lived with her childless sister and brother-in-law in a remote village, the three of them growing old together, scraping a living by collecting firewood and selling it to the villagers. This accounted for her stoop, for she had spent the last twenty-five years bending to pick up pieces of wood. Mr Ali, thousands of miles away in London, was the family's saviour; he sent ten pounds home regularly (my rent money) – enough to feed the three of them for the month. When he heard about her illness he posted an extra ten pounds with which they took her to the nearest doctor, some thirty miles away by bus. The doctor took the ten pounds, examined her, drew blood, inspected it under a microscope, tested her urine sample and finally pronounced her merely fatigued by old age. He gave her a capsule containing about ten differently coloured pills, each of them slightly mildewed, then sent her away. She took ten days rest and one pill a day, at the end of which she felt strong again, getting up on the eleventh day from her bed to collect firewood. On the twelfth day, the same pains started again and continued until Mr Ali sent, three months later, an air ticket so that she could travel to England to rest, eat good food and be looked after by Mrs Ali.

She was my companion in the late hours when she would come upstairs to the toilet adjoining my room and spend an hour there coughing and vomiting. I was awakened by the violence of each upheaval and the groans that followed. I pushed open the toilet door to see her leaning against the wall, dazed and weakened. 'Are you all right?' I asked impotently. She looked at me and summoned up a few words in Urdu. I brought her a glass of water, not knowing what else to do. She took it in her frail hand and swallowed, some of the water running down her mouth and neck. I went away, but could not sleep, feeling the pain in her body and my utter inability to comfort her. Each night, just after midnight, she hauled herself upstairs to the toilet to vomit, and in the intervals I offered her water, orange juice or milk. I always held her hand, and supported her as she returned to her bed. No words passed between us, but a dependency developed as between mother and son, the dying and the living. I stopped going to bed at midnight, reading late into the night, waiting for the sound of footsteps creaking the stairs. I needed her to come upstairs, to continue the relationship, and missed her on those few occasions when she broke the routine, lying awake in my bed wondering desperately whether she had died. Mr Ali was extremely grateful for my late-night vigilance. Whereas previously he had chided me for staying up late and urged me to stop reading and go to bed to save on his electricity bill, now he positively encouraged my studies. I no longer had to contemplate candles, or an oil lamp such as lit the house of my grandmother in Albion Village, to finish off essays. I began to feel sorry for him as I watched his spirit crumbling, his old character of parsimony and bullying undermined by his sister's sickness.

'All for nothing, all this for nothing,' he said on a visit to my room the night after his sister was taken to hospital by ambulance. It was about eight in the evening, I was just about to sit down to eat some food when there was a sudden commotion downstairs, doors opening and slamming and Mrs Ali shouting at the top of her voice. After a few minutes the doorbell rang. I peeped out of my door to see two men in blue uniforms enter, bearing a stretcher. I rushed downstairs, following them into the living-room, where the sister lay crumpled in a ball of bloodied clothing, breathing heavily, moaning. They put her on the stretcher whilst Mrs Ali rushed around, collecting things in a bag, a towel, sari, toothbrush, and Mr Ali stood by the door immobilised by grief and watched them take her out and slide her into the ambulance. As she left through the front door, she looked up, recognised me, tried to raise her hand as if to signal something, to say something, but the men were in a hurry, they put her hand back under the blanket and silenced her with a 'There! there!

you'll be all right dear! There's a good girl, don't wear yourself out, we'll soon get you back on your feet,' whilst I looked into her eyes and smiled weakly as if to reassure her that the two strangers were kindly and at the same time telling her goodbye forever.

'All this for nothing,' he repeated in a mournful voice, gesturing to the walls, the ceiling, the floor. 'Twelve years I come here, work, save, work, buy house, paint, put new window in, new roof, dig up garden, plant vegetables like back home, like farming, all come to nothing.' It was a Friday, rent day, but he had come up to mourn not to collect his dues. When I took out the ten pound note and gave it to him, he held it for a moment, then put it down on the table. 'Money no good for me now, nothing,' he said, obsessed by his sister's illness. He looked at my feet. 'Buy new shoe, how can you walk down road with thing like that?' and he put the note in my hand, his face suddenly glowing with kindness and friendship. 'How your mother and father don't pity you and send things for you?' he asked. He suddenly wanted to find out about my family, as if to drown his own sense of doom.

'What you want to do when you leave school?' he wanted to know.

'Go to university, become a doctor, or a lawyer.'

'Then what?'

'I'm not sure . . . help people, make money, buy a car, buy a house, get married.' He listened intently as I sketched a vague future.

'Then what?'

There was a long silence in which I tried to imagine

the substance of life to come whilst he drifted off into thoughts about his sister's coming death, the funeral arrangements, the gathering of the family, the telephone calls, telegrams, the burial in Balham Cemetery, the drugged sleeping that night and the waking up to horrible cold sunlight, to the echoes of yesterday's prayers and the ritual of shaving, brushing, dressing in mournful clothes to visit the grave for months to come, stopping in at the florists at the top of the road for a fresh wreath, boarding the train and bearing your distress in total privacy in the crowded compartment, unfamiliar people reading newspapers, books, chewing sweets, chatting, no one knowing, and you boxed in your own grief, like a coffin. You look around and wonder how many have felt the same, have suffered the loss, or are about to, and you want to reach out to them, to share something, you don't know exactly what, and to say something which even in your broken English and Paki accent would touch them and inspire responses. Of course you don't. Instead you sit there wedged between strangers, looking at your hands, your feet, fingering your tie, until the train disgorges you onto the platform, all the time wondering why we must live as we die, alone, by ourselves. A bus takes you to the cemetery which is packed with graves, thousands of headstones and concrete mounds, each marking the spot of someone whom you've never seen and never will, and each a stranger to the body beside them. You come to your portion of this vast unknown earth where your sister lies, and spend an hour there crying to yourself, arranging flowers, reading the English words on the headstone for the hundredth time, by now totally fluent in the deciphering of the words.

I fancied that my own immortality was secured by the verse on her tombstone, for when Mr Ali was faced with the problem of an appropriate inscription, it was me he approached to compose a set of words. 'Something that will last,' he said, 'tell her story, that people will forever see what my sister was, and my family.' Joseph's obsession with nothingness came back to me. It was puzzling to conceive how an illiterate peasant woman – draped in rags all her life, next to nothing, who could barely get a visa to enter England, coughing all over her entry forms and the immigration officer at Heathrow so that he moved back slightly from his pillar-shaped desk where he stood like a sentinel, still not escaping the thin spray of blood and spittle, and stamped her passport quickly to get rid of her unpleasant presence – was transformed by death, so that now she was moving freely above clouds, seeing with an astronaut's eye the eeriness of the earth beneath, the blue wash of ocean tides, the green and gold splashes of forests and deserts, the spread of land without boundaries except for gleaming rivers and mountains, and when she looked up, a billion lanterns hanging from the dome of space in a carnival of lights. All the mysteries which hurt our minds yielded up their secrets to her. The mathematics, physics, chemistry and geology of the whole universe she calculated in an instant, she who once could only count according to the number of fingers and toes, wrapping ten twigs at a time in string, each bundle to be sold for one rupee. Now her all-seeing eye traced the hidden underground stream, found the ideal site for the village well, when before she and her brethren dug forlornly in the dust; she discovered a mine of diamond-laden rocks only half a mile from her hut, enough to buy wheat to feed the whole province for the rest of the century. And her mouth, shrivelled with age, barely consolidating some remaining teeth, could now utter the most fluent songs, could quote from a thousand books of literature at will, could speak innumerable languages. For a few daydreaming moments I envied her genius before it all became too foolish to contemplate and the echoes of her vomiting brought me down to earth. The house was silent now that she had gone and the nights lonely. Two weeks in hospital, a flurry of activities downstairs as Mr and Mrs Ali came and went with plastic bags stuffed with samosas, chapatis, fruit, clean clothing, until the telephone rang one afternoon and a cry broke from Mr Ali, a howl that dropped all pretence to civilisation and surrendered to pure instinct. It was during a commercial break, and I turned down the volume on the television and stared mindlessly at the screen, Mr Ali's grief imparting a desolation to the Andrex toilet rolls being advertised by a dog, followed by the meat that nine out of ten cats preferred. I was confused, no longer knowing what mattered. The programme was resumed, some politicians arguing with violent bias about the steep rise of inflation, its dire effects, the bottom dropping out of markets, the plunge into unemployment, loss of prestige, the nation falling apart – none of which mattered any more to Mr Ali who, seized by a sense of loneliness, sobbed automatically, almost objectively.

I gladly took on the project of writing his sister's epitaph, my first venture into poetry, the beginning, I thought excitedly, of a literary career. Although time was short, I set about the task like a professional, asking Mr Ali a series of questions about his sister so as to build up a human profile, a sense of character, setting, plot, mood. There was, however, not much he could tell me about her which I could not guess already: no strange tales or memorable incidents. Either death had blanked his memory or she was truly ordinary. Perhaps he did not care to remember. Still I persisted, seeking to uncover the slightest clue which would lead me to hidden bounties and inspire a treasury of words. But there was no landmark, no strangely lopsided rock, no scratchings in the soil which would suggest secret burials. Her life was as plain as the ground in which the village stood, an expanse of neatly tilled earth, even furrows made by oxen for centuries, the same lines cut open, then sealed, cut open again in a regular succession, the rains coming each November, the crops pushing up in March for harvest in June, then ploughing in September for November's rainfall. The same ragged men trailed behind the same oxen, until they all dropped dead and were replaced by another generation of ragged men and beasts that looked the same, performed the same tasks at the same appointed hours. Or so Mr Ali suggested, refusing to confess intimate details, no doubt numbed by despair. He stared into the electric fire and the two lit bars must have reminded him of firewood because he muttered something about her daily trudge to the forest, which I already knew. 'There must be something else,' I urged as he stared blankly at the fire. But he said nothing more.

Later that night, rain beating against the window-pane, I took up my pen and tried to fabricate verse with an exotic flavour. I imagined a forest swept by monsoon and a child knee-deep in a swamp of leaves searching desperately for dry wood. Buffeted by strong wind the child clutched a small bundle of her livelihood under her arms and struggled homewards, frightened but yet consoled by her haul. Horrid shapes appeared in the semi-darkness, and she tripped over creepers and matted roots as the wind howled savagely and branches reached down from the pitiless gloom to pluck her to devilish regions of air. After a flurry of ideas, ending with the magnificent leap of a man-eating tiger, its stripes burning bright in the forest of the night, I paused in self-doubt, wondering whether I could ever rival Conrad and the other white writers when it came to jungle scenes. True, the story was potentially rich with symbols to do with human vulnerability, delusion, expectations cheated by death, and so on, but I couldn't think beyond the first stanza ('The winds of death that scatter human hope/Dry sticks and barren twigs tied up with rope/Were all the substance of your earthly life/Something something something something knife or wife or strife'). It was more difficult than I thought to find exact rhymes, never mind the phrases to precede them, and it would probably take ten more lines before I had space to fit the tiger in, by which time the grave-stone would have grown two extra feet to accommodate all the words. My thoughts drifted off instead to Janet, I imagined her curled under the blanket like a comma, or, touched by a wisp of dream as ticklish as the tips of my fingers stroking her naked back, she straightened like an exclamation mark and her nipples confronted me like a colon daring me to conclude what I had timidly begun or to explain it away. I knew that I would take the latter course, stumbling and apologetic as usual, unsure of myself. I emerged from all this literary fantasy and nonsense with a real feeling of incompetence. I put pen to paper again, driven this time by a sense of the pity of my life, the uselessness of it, and the words came in a torrent more real than any Indian monsoon:

Hands clasped tight, lips ~~mumbling~~, ~~moving lips~~
That whisper and pray
To ~~vacant~~ unresponsive skies —
Wringing of wrists:
~~But God is an/idea~~ ~~an a mere~~
But God is mere Idea.
Unheard to weep
       even
Not/a pillow of stone on which to sleep
~~The lingering leaden moist mine~~
~~A lingering pregnant heavy leaden earth~~
Unheard to weep
~~Not~~ a pillow of stone on which to sleep
The spirit of the dead
Moves over the stubborn roll of earth
               what
To meet/terror and what dread?
The wind's soft sweep.

The first light of morning trickled in, and I went to sleep exhausted by the melancholy of the writing yet excited by the process of it. I would finish the poem when I awoke.

As soon as I read it aloud to Joseph and Shaz I knew it was all wrong, even silly. Before waiting for their response I pulled out a selection of Milton's verse, flicked through, alighted on 'Lycidas' and declaimed it, as if to drown the banality of what I had written:

> Who would not sing for Lycidas? He knew
> Himself to sing, and build the lofty rhyme.
> He must not float upon his wat'ry bier
> Unwept, and welter to the parching wind,
> Without the meed of some melodious tear.

'Don't stop, don't stop,' Joseph urged to my utter surprise, and I continued into another thirty lines, stumbling over the antique words but being waved on by him until exhausted by the effort. He listened intently to every word, seeming to understand everything, as if the curious diction and phrases held no difficulty of comprehension to one versed in Rasta roots talk.

'You can't apply that rubbish to Mr Ali's sister,' Shaz interrupted Joseph's meditation, 'it's old-fashioned white-people expression.' Like me he was unsure about half the literal sense of Milton's verse, never mind the hidden layers of meaning.

'Is music, man,' Joseph disagreed, 'pure sound. It

ain't got no factory machine noise, no bang, bang, bang, ping, crash, crash or car bark and backfire, nothing in it make of iron and steel and ball-bearings, it ain't got no oil, no grease, no coal, is pure soul.' The printed letters must have appeared to him as beautiful and mysterious as musical notes.

'Pure soul,' he repeated, a glazed look on his face.

'I don't care if it's farted straight from the arse of Angel Gabriel,' Shaz retorted ('the seat of Jove would be more appropriate,' I suggested as a deflationary aside, but he was in full cry), 'you just can't write about Mrs Ali like that.'

'Why not?' Joseph asked, looking at Shaz with disbelief at the latter's refusal to acknowledge the obvious.

'Because she's a little skinny black woman from Pakistan, that's why. Black people have to have their own words.'

'True, there's nothing black about the Milton,' Joseph answered, in the same tone of quiet conviction that always made me trust his judgement, however scatty, before the common-sense of Shaz. 'The thing ain't got no oil stain or diesel fume or char. It ain't concern with industry smoke or making money or progress, that's why the man set it in long time back, all them fairy-tale gods and nymphs. Lycidas dead and gone to a world where nowaday-things don't matter nothing, like white people against black people, like thieving and hustling and pimping and rioting, like slavery and all that kind of history. The man turn pure spirit, pure like flowing water, that's why it's all water talk, the theme thing is water. His body bathe and the spirit come out clean-clean and clear – not white or black but clear. All of we is music, all of we is clear underneath, inside,' he concluded on a note of philosophical triumph, to which Shaz sniggered and said the only sound that was clear were the bells dangling from the fool's cap on Joseph's head. But Joseph was not in the least bothered, it was as if he was addressing himself in an effort at self-explanation, for he suddenly arose from the bed, took up his camera and moved to the door.

'I want to see you tomorrow,' he said in a stern English tone, 'to discuss making another film.'

'Why not now?' I asked, 'don't leave just yet.'

'Because I got to go and think on it deep and come back.'

'Let's talk it through now, I'll make some coffee,' I urged, anxious for him to stay. These days I dreaded being left alone with Shaz and his questions about my sexual progress with Janet. He was becoming obsessed with bodily functions, fired by the possibilities of weird experiments, and he wanted to use me as a sounding-board for his curious ideas. I was, however, determined to compose the epitaph before the night was out, the funeral being a week hence, so as soon as Joseph departed I insisted on continuing the conversation by seeking from him an explanation of his statement that 'black people must have black words.' To me 'black words' meant the language of Albion Village, the vivid curses of Richilo after he had sucked at the mouth of a rum bottle, or the picturesque proverbs of the villagers.

My grandmother's frequent utterance, for instance, was 'one one dutty mek dam,' meaning that every small bit contributed towards making the desired whole, that pennies had to be put aside to make pounds, that nothing was to be wasted or overlooked. She lived her whole life by that motto, saving every scrap of thread, loose buttons, pieces of elastic and coloured paper which she kept in a cardboard box under the bed. I spent a frustrating hour unpicking the knots of the twine which secured the box, but it was a thoroughly worthwhile task rewarded by the discovery of a treasure trove of bric-a-brac. When she was away fetching water or visiting relatives, Peter and I ransacked the box and played all day. We screwed up the coloured paper into the shapes of men, making two armies, one green, one blue, one British, one German. The elastic bands were converted into cannons which fired paper missiles at the paper soldiers. The buttons were tanks which moved eccentrically along the wooden floor of the battlefield according to our skill in flicking them from one strategic position to another. Peter invariably introduced from his bulging pocket novel instruments of defence or destructiveness – a cuckrit seed would serve as a German castle under siege by British soldiers, or a matchbox a prison in which Jews were locked up and suffocated to death and which had to be liberated by the British. We played out these military dramas gleaned greedily from comic books, until real war broke out when Peter tried to introduce Juncha into the arena. Juncha was an old broken-foot Indian who pushed a trolley of sweets up and down the village road. He was hideous to look at, a broad scar running from his forehead and across his nose and cheek, disfiguring the edge of his lips. It was as if the flesh had been gouged out and flattened to form a smooth path along his face. Certainly the insects thought so, for it was not unusual to see an ant or fly moving along the track in his face, never deviating onto the terrain of black skin on either side. I bought a penny fudge and as he bent into his trolley to pick one out I marvelled at the sight of an ant slowly travelling along the scar, lowering its head to lick at a minuscule grain of sugar before moving on. When it reached the end of the scar, instead of venturing into Juncha's stubble, it turned around and headed back up-country in the direction of his nostrils. 'What you staring at, smallboy?' he grunted, lifting the trolley to move on, and without waiting for an answer he stuck out his tongue, moved its tip up and down the scar until he located the ant, swept it into his mouth, chewed, swallowed loudly and belched. I dropped my fudge and ran.

'Ma, who is Mr Juncha and how come he face cut up?' I asked, but as usual she was too busy chopping up firewood to bother with a proper answer.

'He come off the boat from India like that,' she said, taking up a broom to sweep up the bits.

I thought for a while before venturing a second question. 'Ma, you know if he does eat small boys?'

She paused, stood upright, a look of surprise on her face as if I had discovered some terrible secret, then bent again over her broom and swept furiously.

'You don't have to frighten, is only bad boys he does eat,' she declared, pausing again from her work, 'only boy who thief and dunce boy who don't do he school-work.' She looked hard at me, as if daring me to respond.

My head spun as I remembered all the occasions I had stolen money from my mother's purse. 'But how does he know who good from who thief?' I recovered, my voice tinged with desperation and defiance.

'He know what he know,' she answered mysteriously, and resumed her sweeping.

'And I not a dunce either!' I shouted above the noise of the broom, 'so Juncha better watch out if he think he can gobble me up. I go chop the other side of his face if he not careful.'

She paused again. 'You can count?' she challenged.

'From one to two hundred,' I answered stoutly, and without waiting for prompting I began to reel off the numbers. She stopped me when I reached seventeen or thereabouts, and dared me to spell 'mouse'. I did so. 'And "cockroach"?' She put down the broom, took up a bucket of water and went to clean the stairs. I followed her spelling the word aloud. 'And "centipede"? And "mosquito"? And "snake"? And "woodworm"?' I stood at the top of the stairs spelling and watched her slowly move down from board to board. She scrubbed and wiped, as if to banish all the pests and hazards she was asking me to spell.

'J-J-Juncha get cut up in w-w-white m-man war long time back,' Peter insisted, 'I g-g-go make he a g-g-general.' He tied a piece of red string around the top of a twig, signifying a bloody bandage around Juncha's forehead and face.

'But Ma say he fight-up drunk and curse in boat and the other coolie people chop he across he mouth,' I protested, 'the man is rascal not soldier.'

'You Ma h-h-hignorant, how she go k-k-know,' he retorted.

The insult stung me. I scattered his soldiers, picked up the twig and snapped it. 'Your Ma is ugly whore, no wonder you Papa left she and run way with another woman.'

Peter was stunned. His face creased up as if it was going to cry. I immediately felt sorry for what I had done. I rearranged his soldiers and shot a sheep-dung pellet at them, but Peter was not playing, sulking a few yards off, eyes lowered. I fired another pellet, this time from Peter's side, at my own soldiers, knocking two over. This time he looked up, budging a little. 'You bound to win the war,' I said in a mock-distressed voice to entice him back to the game, scanning the battlefield and calculating the advantage in men he had over me. I flicked a pellet carelessly in the direction of his soldiers, knowing I would miss. 'Your turn,' I said, a note of fabricated desperation in my voice as I contemplated my defeat. After a little while he came up and aimed a volley of sheep-dung in my direction, killing practically all my men. I surrendered. Glee returned to his face. 'You really know Juncha is soldier-man?' I asked as we put the coloured paper and string back into Ma's box.

'Yes, man, I t-t-telling you.'

'But how you know?'

'I a-a-ask he and h-h-he tell me.'

I was astonished. 'You mean you talk to he, you not afraid he go eat you?'

Peter laughed.

'But you can't spell, how he don't gobble you up?'

'De man don't f-f-frighten me,' he said bravely, 'I know w-w-what to do.' He bunched his fingers, put them in his mouth and bit, holding in his breath as long as possible. He explained to me that it was the greatest cure for fright. No one could harm you once you performed that act. It worked always, no matter who was threatening you and whatever the circumstances of your peril. 'And I can s-s-spell as well,' he added defiantly when I scoffed at his superstitious country belief.

Later that day, Juncha limped along the road, pushing his wheelbarrow and ringing his bell. A few small boys dropped their cricket bat and ball, scooted out of the yard to buy sweets. Peter and I were on the highest branches of a star-apple tree, eating fruit and swinging recklessly in a strong wind. 'Let's go get jilabie,' I told him. I climbed down expertly and waited for him at the bottom of the tree. It seemed to take ages for him to descend and I was anxious in case Juncha moved on. He manoeuvred his fat body clumsily, getting himself wedged in forks, and climbing out with the greatest of effort. 'Let's go,' I urged as he landed with a thud, jumping from a low branch.

'You g-g-go, I hurt me foot,' he replied, stooping and rubbing his ankle. There was fright in his eyes.

153

'You foot alright man, come quick.'

'I ain't got m-m-m-mon-m-m-mon-,' he stammered endlessly, his tongue siezed to an unaccustomed degree.

I fished out a bright penny from my pocket. 'I go pay if you buy the jilabie from Juncha,' I bribed him.

He opened his mouth to say something but it took a full minute for him to utter the words 'I ain't hungry, I eat too much star-apple already.' I was dumbfounded by his refusal of sweets. He looked at me piteously, as if begging mercy for his cowardice, and curled his body in an attitude of surrender. My sisters and I once trapped a mouse in a shoe-box. We boiled the kettle to scald it to death, but when we lifted the cover the mouse looked up at us, frozen in terror, then began to shiver. It curled its head to its chest, and its whole body shook. It was obviously begging for its life by showing us how powerless it was, but we poured the water over it nevertheless. Now, as I saw Peter cowering before me I wanted to forgive him, to let him go, but found myself laughing at him instead. I put my fingers in my mouth and bit, mocking him. It was the most natural thing in the world to hurt him. 'I go tell all the other boys,' I shouted in his ears. He covered his face with his arms to hide the tears, 'You're a fat, stupid, ugly, country coolie,' I cursed, and picked up a stick to lash his head.

'Death heals the wound of life,' I wrote. 'Delivers us from the fury and strife/More cleanly than any midwife/

More skilful than the surgeon's knife/It leaves no scar, no hideous – ,' before petering out for want of a final rhyme. All this talk of wounds and knives reminded me of Nasim in his hospital bed, and the image of his helpless, immigrant body punctured a last attempt to soar poetically. I felt like Joseph's paper bag, leaking air. I screwed up the poem, bored by the project of universalising the petty death of Mr Ali's sister. Everything was petty, Mr Ali, his family, Peter, myself, and words were only ways of falsifying the pettiness, words were a fancy lie. When Joseph arrived early next morning, I unscrewed the various pieces of paper on which were scribbled elevated words and read them to him. The act of reading them aloud immediately revealed their mediocrity.

Joseph diverted me by his own elaborate plans to film the funeral. It would be a more powerful statement on the old woman's life than any epitaph I could compose, he assured me. Once a silent admirer of books which I used to read aloud to him, he was now bold in his belief in the superiority of images, his increasing familiarity with the camera leading to a certain arrogance of outlook. He was no longer impressed by my erudition, and even thought the Conrad a poor work since it contained little material that could be converted into visuals. He judged every book now according to its potential for film treatment, brushing aside my clever analysis of literary texture. I consoled myself that he still needed me to write the film script, only to find that he had abolished me in his latest plans for the funeral. I was, originally, to 'front' the film, like a BBC commentator at state funerals. As the hearse left the parlour I was to turn my face in its direction, watching it move slowly towards the cemetery half a mile away. The camera would track its dignified progress. Then with doleful expression, I would turn to the camera, the hearse receding in the distance, and utter slow, sombre words on the tragedy of human life, ending with the only Latin I knew, 'sunt lachrimae rerum'. As soon as Shaz shouted 'cut', we would scramble after the hearse on foot, hoping to catch up with it before it deposited its coffin in the hole. Shaz put his bicycle at our disposal in case I fluffed my speech and needed to do it again and we ran over schedule. Joseph was to gather up his camera, perch on the bar and be cycled furiously after the hearse by Shaz. I would catch up as best I could. Joseph would then film the prayers beside the grave, the tears flowing from people's faces, the sobbing, the lowering of the coffin. At this point I would have arrived panting into the cemetery. Joseph had calculated that it would take me twenty minutes to run all the way. He would give me ten minutes to recover my breath, during which time the mourners would have turned to go and the grave-diggers taken up their spades. As soon as the first load of gravel rattled on the coffin board, I was to address the camera with my rehearsed speech, a final sweep of poetic words.

His new plans disposed of me, and I listened sullenly as he outlined them. He babbled excitedly about putting together a montage of images. The idea was highly ambitious, no less than a complete statement of the condition of England. There would be no verbal commentaries nor connecting narrative, and the images would be accompanied by natural sounds. It began with a stone thrown into water, the rippling outwards that eventually petered out and was absorbed into stillness. Joseph said that this signified the Act of Creation itself, and all movements that followed, the movements of the stars, of the earth through the stars, of the rise of man from slime and fish and mammal and of the journeying of man across rivers and oceans, all of which mighty effort ended in death and stillness. Further extravagant images followed, each crammed with layers of meaning.

'A film is like mirror,' he explained, 'everybody who watch it see something different but is not necessarily what they want to see. They can't just make up what it is they see, but they all still see different.'

I nodded wisely at this weighty piece of philosophy as he proceeded to describe how all the action was to emanate from a human body and for this purpose he would enlist the help of one of the tramps in Clapham Common. The camera would picture the blackened tramp lying drunkenly in the grass, then zoom in as he coughed and spat. The image of white phlegm flying from his mouth would give way to a shot of Concorde moving across a wide sky. Then the tramp's hand fumbled about his pocket and produced a bundle of confetti which he would fling angrily into the air; it would flutter down like many coloured butterflies. The hand, agitated by memories, would claw at the earth, removing top soil and delving deeper until it discovered a child's tooth which it held up to the sun to examine like a precious stone. Suddenly the tooth became covered in a film of oil. The tramp cried aloud and rubbed it frantically on his sleeve but the tooth only became blacker. The wind blew a piece of scrap paper from somewhere and the tramp caught it and wrapped the tooth in it. The paper was a letter someone had crumpled up and thrown away. All the words were smudged in mud beyond recognition, except a half line written in bold letters: I COMING HOME SOON, O.K. He set light to the paper and put it to the tooth, as if to burn off the oil. A huge flame arose, fed by the oil, but when it died down, the tooth was as black as ever. The tramp fumbled in his other pocket and found a white door-knob with a black key stuck in it. He tried to turn the key, one way, then the other, but the key wouldn't budge. He threw the lot away, reached into his pocket again and took out what looked like a five-pound note. On closer inspection the camera revealed that it was a worthless piece of paper on which the tramp, using crayons, had coloured in lines and patches of blues, greys and pinks, in imitation of the appearance of a five-pound note. He had also redrawn the images: Queen Elizabeth and her bejewelled crown were replaced by a Rastafarian with locks sprouting under a red, green and yellow beret. The Duke of Wellington's arms were no longer folded: he held a whip over the naked body of a black woman and his eyes bulged as he beheld the chains wrapped erotically around her neck, breasts and ankles.

'But where is all this leading to, what's the story behind it?' I asked after he had reeled off half a dozen more bizarre images which culminated with a stream of black ants carrying flecks of food, making their way up the chest and neck of the tramp and disappearing into his nostrils only to be trapped in a mat of hair and sneezed out violently (this last image signified the experience of immigration: the black ants were West Indians laden with suitcases landing on the tarmac of England, and the nostrils were the interrogation lounges at Heathrow). He ignored my question, as if it were too trivial to command an answer.

'I want my film bury in the coffin of Mr Ali sister,' he declared, 'so one day, five hundred years or five thousand years from now when they dig her up they'd see who she really is.'

I must have looked puzzled because he proceeded to offer a more detailed explanation. According to Joseph, there was no point making a realistic film with an ordinary story which had a beginning and an end, because in the distant future the film would have no meaning. Both Mr and Mrs Ali would have been dead, the house they lived in would have been demolished, the street changed, indeed the whole physical structure of the city would have been totally altered. People in five centuries hence watching the film of an Asian couple in Cherry Street, Balham, London, in the 1970s would not be able to make even basic sense of what they were seeing, except if they had an expert historian or scholar to interpret it for them. Even Asian people might no longer exist; not just the saris but the brown skin itself: because of nuclear war or changes in the atmosphere people in the year 2500 may be green or bright pink. Mr Ali's sister, simple as she was to us, would be the most complex creature to fathom five hundred years from now. The thing to do, therefore, was to make a new language with film which would not alter with time, a language which told about journey, loss, rejection and death not by describing particular episodes or characters but by using what he called 'a set of open-ended symbols'. The jargon impressed me. By some mysterious process the possession of a camera led to his picking up a technical vocabulary, so that these days he would effortlessly drop words like 'super-8 definition' and 'splicing' into our conversations. Although I was doubtful of the feasibility of the project, I was filled with admiration at how ambitious it was, how touched with genius. How, I wondered, could a rough-looking Rastaman who thought sentences were things handed out by magistrates, and who couldn't decipher a single word on a page, come up with such images? I wished for a moment that I had the freedom of his ignorance, his irresponsibility. As it was I had essays to compose in the normal way, proper books to read, exams to take, a future to chart out. I couldn't afford to take risks as he could. He had no desire to make something of his life, no desire to own and possess things by sheer hard work, to arrive at somewhere by the sheer application of workable ideas. The social-welfare system had nurtured him from birth and would do so until he died. I wanted to make my own way by my own skill and strength.

Not surprisingly Mr Ali would have none of Joseph's film, and was horrified when I asked him permission to bury it in his sister's coffin. He was agitated and wanted to ban Joseph from his house. Fortunately I had samples of verse to offer him and I lied by saying that Joseph had helped me to compose them. This calmed him down. He read what I had written, struggling to control his emotions as he suddenly remembered that his sister at that very moment was lying in the hospital fridge.

'Is this best you can do?' he asked, re-reading the samples. A new sadness overcame him, this time provoked by a dissatisfaction with my efforts. 'Can't you write something more about who she was, how she look, how she live?' he wanted to know.

I felt insulted and went on the offensive. 'Epitaphs are only meant to express general sorrow, Mr Ali. You can't say anything precise in them, you can't give details.'

'Why not?' he demanded.

I was at a loss for an answer, unless I offered Joseph's argument about the meaninglessness of today's words and images five centuries from now. Only Joseph could explain his theory in his own rambling nonsensical way. If I tried I would sound absurd and pretentious. It struck me that another way of putting it would be to point to the heap of bones that all corpses become, all the same colour and all anonymous. Mrs Ali's sister would soon decompose to an unrecognisable mess, so what did the details of her appearance, her habits, her specific life, matter? The epitaph needed to be as universal as her bones. As soon as this idea came to me I knew I couldn't express it because the truth of his sister's fate, the very imagining of the way worms would arise in her flesh, the way it would loosen and leak, would distress him. I evoked literary precedents instead, telling him of how Shakespeare did them, and Wordsworth. 'Epitaphs are open-ended symbols you know,' I concluded. He looked at me, wanting to query what I meant by this, but said nothing because he was ashamed of appearing to be ignorant.

'You sure Shakespeare sound like what you write on this piece of paper?'

I assured him of the closeness of the imitation.

'And what about other man – Saucer or what his name is, the man from Canterbury?' he persisted.

I told him that Chaucer would have written the same, except in old-time English. That seemed to have satisfied him for he reached into his pocket and gave me five pounds for my verse. I made a pretence of refusing it, pressing it back into his hand, but he insisted, so I took it. There was more to it than greed as I slipped the money into my pocket: I felt a real sense of achievement, of arrival, like a proper writer receiving his first down-payment.

Joseph was demolished when I broke the news to him. I offered him a chocolate biscuit in the hope of softening the blow but he just sat there, staring at his shoes, the camera lying abandoned in his lap.

'It's not you, it's just that Muslims have their own rituals and beliefs and we can't just film their funerals like that,' I tried to explain, but he was set in his gloom, chewing the biscuit without tasting it.

'What are you going to do now,' I asked.

'I don't know,' he said, looking forlornly at the camera. I reached and picked it up, examined the dials, twiddled with the lens, peered through the aperture, as a way of renewing my friendship with him.

'It must be difficult to operate this thing,' I offered and waited for an answer.

'Not really,' he said, in a tired voice, knowing that I was only trying to flatter him, to bolster his confidence. 'To be truthful, I don't understand it myself, I'm useless really . . .'

His confession saddened me. I wanted him to keep up his interest and not lose heart. I liked the way he held the camera to his face and pointed it at trees, tramps, traffic, as if to give meaning to them, as if without his selection and recording these things and people would not matter.

The camera in turn gave him status and importance, it made him visible whenever he was out filming, a small crowd always gathering out of curiosity. His bravado helped me to escape from the sense of my own smallness. I had talent, but relative to the huge world outside, relative to the billions of people who have lived from the beginning of time and are still living, I was nothing special, just another life occupying a brief space. Perhaps the talent I had in analysing literature was only a mechanical trick anyway, that anyone with patience and effort could learn and excel at. Joseph was now putting down his camera and seeing himself for what he was, and I was afraid for him, and for myself. 'Is only boasting to you and Shaz I been doing,' he confessed, 'many times I press the wrong buttons or just guess at which one I should press. The only thing I'm good at is getting to jail and breaking out of jail.'

*   *   *

I thought of his words as Shaz and I hurried to his hideout with our plastic bag of crisps, apples and lemonade. Someone had called the police, and they had arrested him on a Tuesday afternoon in most peculiar circumstances, and with the greatest of difficulty, for Joseph was high up an oak tree in Tooting Bec Common, at least thirty feet from the ground, dangling dangerously by the waist. He had tied a rope around his body, secured it on the branch, braced his feet against the trunk and pointed his camera skyward, filming the wind as it brushed the leaves of the uppermost branch. Whoever spotted him must have thought he was about to commit suicide. Before long a police car mounted the pavement and roared across the grass. A small crowd gathered. Joseph was oblivious to all this drama, so intent was he on the challenge of capturing on film the invisibility of wind. A policeman barked an order into a megaphone. Joseph looked down, startled by the sudden noise. His feet slipped, his body fell and swung on the rope, the branch creaked as if about to break, and the camera dropped from his hand. A shriek escaped his mouth, he kicked and struggled as if to loosen himself and plunge down after the camera. The policeman shouted at him to keep calm, to untie the rope and to come down, but he remained suspended by the waist, a look of extreme alarm on his face. He knew that he would be arrested once they made enquiries and discovered that the camera was stolen. The policeman radioed for help and before long a fire engine drove up to the scene. A ladder slid upwards, a fireman balanced on

164

the rungs, until it reached ten feet from where Joseph was hanging.

'What do you think you are playing at?' the fireman shouted, 'grip the rope and pull yourself up to the branch.'

Joseph looked at him without saying anything.

'Are you deaf or what? Grip the rope, I haven't got all day,' the fireman said.

'Leave me alone,' Joseph replied calmly. He pulled out a knife from his back pocket and put its blade against the rope, telling the fireman to send the camera up right away, otherwise he'd cut the rope and make a big mess all over the grass. The fireman, shocked by this unexpected development, hurried down, muttering something about monkeys. After a short, agitated conversation with the policeman, he was hoisted up again, bearing the camera which Joseph graciously took from him, thanking him for his kindness. He slung it around his shoulder, re-positioned himself against the tree and resumed his filming. The fireman descended and took his place among the crowd straining to catch sight and make sense of the black figure high up in the tree. An hour elapsed during which most of the people, sensing the absence of further drama, gave up and went their way, and only the policeman, the fireman and a few children remained. Boredom set in. The policeman, at first utterly murderous at Joseph's arrogance and disobedience, reporting agitatedly to base or shouting threats through his megaphone, now settled down to await the inevitable descent. After all there were more unpleasant tasks to be done; better to leave those to his colleagues and to bide his time in the Common where occasionally young women would pass by on whose bodies he could fantasise for a while, thus making the wait more tolerable. He turned off his flashing beacon, wrote out the arrest card, chatted with the fireman about the latest pay increase.

'You look like an animal,' Shaz said bluntly as he devoured an apple. He was crouched over a fire which he had started from bits of wood and paper. His face was bruised and his clothing soiled. He unscrewed the top of the lemonade bottle and guzzled down the lot as if he had been without liquid for days. I watched him eat through two packets of crisps, all the while fascinated by his abominable condition. His hideout was a half-demolished brick house in a Balham back street. In the semi-darkness I imagined rats crawling around the broken timbers, pools of water, pieces of abandoned furniture. Shaz wanted to know how he had escaped from prison but he merely stared wildly at us and muttered 'the camera, the camera' over and over. We left him and promised to return the next day with more food and a blanket. He said nothing, retreating into the darkness of the far corner of the room where we heard him talking to himself about 'film', 'the lens mash up', 'the parts need oiling'.

When Janet visited that Sunday I had truly exciting news to tell her, and the fact that Shaz and I were accessories to Joseph's crime gave an added relish to my description of it. For once in my life I was engaged in something seriously illegal and I took advantage of my situation to deluge her with details of his battered face, his fractured leg from climbing over a thirty-foot prison wall and huge rats crawling around his hideout. She was appalled and so distracted that the tea that I made her went cold in her hands, the biscuits barely nibbled. I felt a showman of words, the phrases flowed extravagantly. Now that she was enthralled by my power of storytelling all there was to do was to lean towards her intent face and kiss her. But there was an obstinate terror in my mind. I heard my voice babbling on as if controlled by another self, and all the time my mind was desperately trying to compose itself for an assault on her body. In the end it gave way to the terror and only words remained, running on and on like some well-oiled machine, like Joseph's camera.

'Joseph must get some help; what shall we do?' she wanted to know, suddenly identifying with our world. There was such pity in her voice that I felt ashamed of my lust for her. I mumbled something about getting him more food. She volunteered to steal some of her father's clothing for him. She would bake a pie with her mother and take it to him. Whereas Shaz and I had been excited by Joseph's predicament, she was sober in her response, there was not the least evidence of surreptitious pleasure or perverse curiosity. She genuinely wanted to know how we lived as a people, where we came from, where we were heading. The village in Kent where she had been brought up was a stable community. Everyone seemed to know everyone else, all were neighbours. There was a church which was crowded each Sunday, a school where all the children attended, growing up, playing and studying together, until they went off to universities, and a centuries-old village hall where the neighbours sat in neat rows to discuss the maintenance of street lamps. The photographs she showed me revealed that much. I fingered them in a mood of sullen envy. Our lives were messy by contrast: families scattered across the West, settling in one country or another depending on the availability of visas; we lived from hand to mouth, hustling or thieving or working nightshifts and sleeping daytime; we were ashamed of our past, frightened of the present and not daring to think of the future. When I looked at the images of her mother and father in their neat house and manicured garden the first instinct was to inflict pain, to shatter the security of their lives, for in some vague way I felt they were responsible for my own disordered existence. Shaz had been inciting me for the past week with his sex magazines. He was building up a collection, spending all his pocket money at the newsagents. He boasted that Monica was turned on by the pictures, that all women wanted was to be mauled. As proof he read out the letters page of one magazine. One woman confessed to being bored with her job as a solicitor's secretary and described her fantasies of being tied up and taken in a slum alleyway; another, signed 'bored housewife', told of being seduced by a common electrician and his mate as they came to repair a socket in her home, her husband, a rich oil executive, being out of the country on some important business. The men had her repeatedly, their roughness and crude vocabulary giving her multiple orgasms. Afterwards she gave them some of her husband's belongings – his expensive cigarette lighter, a silk scarf, a pocket calculator – as a way of getting her own back for his sexual indiscretions. These stories influenced the way I felt towards Janet so that now, as she sat on my bed going through the photographs, I wondered whether she too wanted to be degraded, whether she really wanted me to stop talking, and to pounce on her instead, smearing blackness over all that genteel Englishness. I wondered how her parents would react if she returned home bruised and bitten and impregnated, whether they would expel her from their presence or protect her by buying me off.

'I don't think you should visit Joseph,' I told her.

'Why not?' she asked, surprised by my sudden decisiveness.

'He doesn't know you, he might think you'll betray him to the police,' I lied.

She looked hurt and rejected.

'Don't take it personally, he's funny that way,' I reassured her. The truth was that I didn't want to involve her in the squalor of Joseph's life, the fraudulence of it. I didn't want her to see the slum basement, to breathe the stench of it, to soil her dress and hands in the dust and leaking water. I wanted to protect her from the dirt of Shaz's magazines. Deep down I preferred to believe in her photographs, I wished I belonged to her family and the village she came from with all its protections and confident virtues.

Shaz scoffed at my confession, calling me bookish and romantic. 'This is the real thing,' he said, holding up a glossy spread of a woman before my eyes, 'can't you just smell that?' I gazed weakly at the picture. 'Don't you just want to cream that doll's face? Joseph is right, man, you got to let go and plunge down on her and don't give a damn where you end up.' He was mocking me, but there was also an intensity in his voice which frightened me. 'Have you done Janet yet?' he asked, laughing, knowing that I had not. I hated the way his tone had changed since he became a magazine addict. There was a new aggression, a monosyllabic grunt of clit, prick, jerk. It was like the sound of his guitar as he practised hopelessly on it, producing sharp, disconnected noise. 'She's not fragrant you know, your Janet. If you poke your finger in her and pull it out you'll see the red slime under your fingernails. They bleed you know, they smell.' I listened to him, overcome with disgust and a sense of his truthfulness. The thought of blood leaking from her as from a broken gutter, soaked up by cotton wool which she flushed down the toilet, reddening the water, made me nauseous.

Joseph was curled up in a ball of dirt when we arrived to hand over our plastic bags. When he raised his head, he looked like a gollywog, his woolly locks spread out in spikes. Shaz greeted him loudly, snapping a chocolate bar in two and handing him a piece. I gave him his guitar which I had rescued from his room. He took it quietly, strummed a few idle notes, adjusted the head and put it aside. He was more listless than usual. The guitar was redundant, all he wanted was the camera. Monica strolled around the basement as if wholly at home in the mess. She had come along to satisfy a vague curiosity, to 'have a peek' as she put it. Bedford Hill was in fact only a few streets away; every night around seven Shaz dropped her off there in a taxi and collected her again around midnight. She looked around Joseph's hideout as if contemplating using it for business in place of the usual deserted garages that men took her to. 'How did you come to know Janet?' I asked her as we walked down Balham High Street on our way to see Joseph. The two of them were complete opposites: Janet had a gentle manner and voice, she wore skirts and dresses which gave a softness to her appearance; Monica was firm-breasted, her hair cropped in an aggressive way, and she wore tight-fitting jeans and sexy ankle boots. She smelled of perfume, chewing gum and rubber. Even with her clothes on she had the same tempting sexuality as the models in Shaz's magazines.

'I live down her street, why?' Monica answered, her eyes gleaming with wickedness.

'Monica's father is an accountant,' Shaz interceded proudly, sensing that I held her in low esteem. He put his arms around her waist as if to protect her from my base desire. I felt uncomfortable in their presence, and paused to look into a shop window, examining the prices of some vacuum cleaners, whilst they walked

171

ahead feeling up each other and giggling shamelessly in broad daylight. I trailed behind, enjoying the sight of her shapely buttocks in blue jeans all the way to Joseph's hideout.

Shaz boasted of his enjoyment of her, sparing no detail in recounting how he threw her on the bed and tore off her clothing. Apparently she liked it rough and sudden, begging him to pull her hair and bite her flesh. The language of his descriptions was straight out of the magazines, so well read was he in 'Confessions of a Randy Housewife' stories and the like. He told me of how she gasped and moaned as he pushed three fingers in and frigged her fast, how she took his knob in her mouth, how he shafted her up to the hilt. His new fluency was a complete transformation from his previous stumbling over the English language as represented in our Chaucer and Conrad examination texts. He no longer bothered me to explain phrases like 'byraft of ech welfare/I bounden in the blake bark of care' or more modern words like 'expatiate' or 'metamorphosis'. He abandoned his studies altogether, his new-found confidence in expression backed up by money accumulated from handling Monica's affairs.

'Come with me to the hospital,' he urged me one day.

'What's the matter?' I wanted to know.

'Man's trouble,' he said, smiling proudly, 'that Italian slag gave me an itch, I've got to get it checked out.' He had called round the previous week and persuaded me to accompany him to the West End where, he said, he had to purchase a special set of magazines. 'And what are you reading now?' he asked, as I put down the book and reached for my jacket. I was labouring over *Troilus and Criseyde*, reading an essay on Criseyde's character. 'You love this rubbish, eh?' he laughed, 'you'll end up an old professor wanking by the fireside, putting aside your pipe and warming up your hand first.' I looked at him sternly. 'Only a joke, man,' he said with mocking reassurance, 'only a joke.' I sat on the bus deep in thought, trying to work out why she should have betrayed him so easily, why after all those pure, shy exchanges, the secret glances, desperate kisses, aching hearts, poetic letters swearing honour and devotion, the desire to lay down fortune and life for the sake of love, why she should have abandoned him for Diomede. It's not enough to say that we're human, I thought, there must be something more than us, some higher quality that we can also possess if we willed it, believed it. I knew what Shaz's response would have been: she was a cunt that Troilus dreamed over and his imagination refashioned into a pool of pure rain-water, flecks of diamond glittering from below the surface as he leaned over to admire his face. But she was only a cunt-doll, just another pussy – salty and oozing and begging for Knight Diomede's prick to lance her. In the end she wanted to be frigged, not fondled by a gentle Troilus or smooched at with his wet words. What Troilus needed was to catch a rash and be a man.

We got off at Piccadilly Circus, headed down some

backstreets and came to an area littered with sex shops, massage parlours and cinemas. It was a wonderland of coloured lights flicking on and off in shop windows, amusement arcades packed with machines that flashed and uttered electronic sounds, and large billboards of women offering their naked flesh to us. The proprietors stood in doorways beckoning us in, bawling out their wares of peepshow girls, striptease, videos, toys. Shaz moved through this playground with ease, stepping over the odd drunk sprawled across the pavement, weaving between the bags of rubbish put out by restaurants, winking at the girls waiting at street corners. I followed raggedly, squirming with self-consciousness, staring ahead as if I was an innocent traveller on my way to another destination.

'Come on,' he turned around and shouted as I passed a shop window, trying to catch sight of the display from the corner of my eye. Guilt quickened my steps and I caught up with him. We turned into another street and crossed over to a sex shop, Shaz's local. He entered confidently, not pausing to look left or right as I did in case someone saw me. I saw nothing as I entered, putting on a serious face and looking at the floor, the walls, at Shaz, anywhere but at the racks of magazines and sex toys. I stayed close to him, out of fright, as he lined up with the other male customers and thumbed through the magazines. I picked one up idly and flicked the pages, again seeing nothing. After a while I put it down and picked up another, not wanting to appear too engrossed in one article, for the proprietor was staring in our direction. Shaz glanced over, saw the pictures and immediately took the magazine from my hand, putting it back on the shelf. 'That's for queers, can't you see! They'll think we're a couple of poofs,' he whispered. I looked at the magazine cover and noticed the photograph of one man leaned over a bench with another man spanking him. He reached for the rack and pushed another magazine in my hand. 'Relax, relax,' he urged under his breath as I fumbled with the pages. It was full of pictures of a black woman standing imperiously over a white man, lying on a sofa, who was trussed up with ropes, chains and blindfolds. I could feel my shyness waning. Sight returned to my eyes. Five minutes had elapsed since we entered the shop, and the longer we stayed, the more secure I felt. I put back the magazine and wandered around to the next rack without waiting for Shaz to accompany me. It was crammed with mysterious devices. I picked up a box of plastic spheres shaped like eggs and read the instructions, marvelling at the language of the blurb, which promised excitement beyond the grasp of the wildest imagination. I wished I could write like that.

There was a peepshow at the far corner of the shop with three individual booths occupied by men, their feet fidgeting against the curtain. As soon as one of the booths was free I slipped in, reached into my pocket and drew out some coins. I wasn't sure what to do. I felt about blindly for some slot and to my great relief found one beside the aperture. I waited a while for my eyes to get accustomed to the darkness and searched the area around the slot for further instructions. There were none. Out of desperation and fearful that there was probably a queue of impatient men behind me, I slipped some coins into the slot, small ones to begin with, so as not to overpay, but as the aperture did not open, I ventured a ten-pence coin, then another and another. Still nothing happened. I looked forlornly at the few coins left in my hand, some twenty-five pence, enough for the busfare home and a cup of tea. What to do? I had already used up a small fortune, there were at least four days before the next social-security cheque arrived and in the meanwhile I had only two pounds at home to buy food. I lingered in the booth, calculating, knowing that it was better to cut my losses by leaving. I pressed my ears against the steel wall, hoping at least to hear what the woman behind was doing since I could not see her. In a fit of desperate desire I put my remaining coins in. The aperture remained obstinately closed. I imagined that I could hear mocking laughter from the woman behind the wall. I searched frantically in my pocket, found my doorkey and pressed its sharp edge against the aperture, trying to force it open. It slipped against the steel with a screeching noise. I froze, expecting any moment that an alarm would go off, the lights would be switched on and I would be dragged out and humiliated in full view of all the customers in the shop. I waited a few seconds, nauseous with fright, composed myself in a massive effort of will, pushed aside the curtain and walked blindly towards Shaz.

'What's up?' he asked, on the night bus back, 'why so quiet and miserable?' It was crowded with young blacks and I sat huddled against the window, wanting to disappear from the sight of the white people who glanced scornfully at them as they talked or laughed loudly, swearing or swilling canned beer. The young males were fashionably dressed, returning from discos and parties. Girls sat on their laps giggling and squirming. An empty beer can flew from the back of the bus to the front, hitting one of the boys on his head and rattling on the floor. There was a roar of laughter, a girl leaned over and kissed his head and his mouth as if to comfort him. He grabbed her breasts and rubbed them together in mock lust. The laughter erupted again, with a few obscenities in Jamaican slang. The handful of whites, mostly late-night workers, women manning cinema kiosks, or office cleaners, put on blank faces, suppressing their indignation and distress. The blacks disregarded them completely, as if thick-skinned, indifferent to other people's opinions. I wished they would behave, act respectfully, keep quiet, read a book, anything, instead of displaying such vulgar rowdiness. No wonder they're treated like animals, I heard myself thinking, distancing myself from all this noisy West Indian-ness, and feeling sympathy for the outnumbered whites. They should send them back home. All they do is dance and breed. Not one 'O' level between a bus-load of them and yet they complain they've got no jobs, no proper housing, no future. If they stayed home and studied, they'd get somewhere. But no, it's dance hall and shiny shoes and expensive clothes. I'm different really. I come from their place, I'm dark-skinned like them, but I'm different, and I hope the whites can see that and separate me from that lot. I'm an Indian really, deep down I'm decent and quietly spoken and hard-working and I respect good manners, books, art, philosophy. I'm like the whites, we both have civilisation. If they send immigrants home, they should differentiate between us Indian people and those black West Indians. I was glad I was sitting next to Shaz, one of my own, with brown skin and straight hair.

It was in this mood of glum contemplation that he disturbed me with his question.

'I'm broke,' I answered him.

'Oh? but you didn't spend any money in the shop, unless' – he looked at me mischievously – 'you've got something hidden under your jumper.' He poked my jacket pocket, feeling my folded plastic raincoat. 'Are you sure that's not a blow-up sex doll in there?' I pulled my pocket away. 'Only joking. Don't get touchy. There's nothing wrong with all that stuff you know, it's fun, it's why we're living. I don't know why people feel guilty or terrified.' We sat quietly for a while. I knew he was wrong, that there was more to life than fun, but I was too tired to think it out and formulate an answer in words. 'I'll lend you a fiver if you want,' he offered, and without waiting for my response, he fished out a wad of notes and peeled off two. 'Here, take ten, I've got loads.' I'd never seen so much cash in my life. He must have been holding a hundred pounds in his hands. 'It's Monica's money,' he said, seeing the astonished expression on my face, 'she makes twice that in a week sometimes. I give thirty pounds a week to my Mum to help her with the mortgage. She thinks I work part-time at nights when I take Monica out. That's more than what my Dad can give her on his wages. I give ten pounds to my sister who's at college doing science.' It was as if he wanted to reassure me that he was in moral control of his actions, that he still retained an Asian sense of duty to his family. 'Everything in this country is about money,' he said, suspecting that I still disapproved of his behaviour, 'you don't want to be a Paki all your life. Here, take it,' and he shoved the notes in my pocket.

The bus rounded a corner unexpectedly and one of the black boys sitting on the seat beside us lost his balance and pushed his hand roughly on my shoulder to steady himself. 'Sorry mate,' he apologised, 'you alright?' I nodded faintly. 'Here,' he said, fishing out a packet of cigarettes from his jacket, 'have one.' 'It's alright,' I mumbled. 'No, no, have one, honest,' he insisted. I took it and put it in my pocket, saying I would smoke it later. The small gesture of friendship made me feel deeply ashamed of myself. I didn't seem to know what to think anymore. Everything was so complicated, all this sudden hate and sudden companionship. I felt dirty when I remembered the way I had groped blindly in the booth for a brief view of breasts, and the feeling of helplessness and poverty when the aperture refused to budge. Nothing will work in my life, I thought, all this reading of books and effort at learning will lead nowhere. I imagined Mr Ali's sister trapped in her coffin as I was in the dark booth, like the walled-in whore.

*   *   *

'I'm no spring chicken love,' the woman warned him on the phone, 'I'm no baby doll,' but he was too desperate for sex to heed her, making a firm appointment as soon as he selected from her menu of prices. He had plucked her number from the special magazine bought at the sex shop. I was beside myself with excitement as we crammed into the telephone box to make contact. Shaz was acting as if he were a veteran of such dealings, pressing the coin resolutely in the slot and putting on a bold voice when she answered. The preliminary conversation was courteous, as if he were transacting some normal business: 'Hello, I'm phoning about your ad in the *Nationwide Contact*, can you give me more details please,' to which she replied, 'Yes, what do you wish to know?' 'How much is it?' he asked. I pressed my ears against the back of the phone to pick up the reply. She started off with the cost of normal services, four pounds for a hand-job, six for straight sex, eight for a blow; then reeled off figures for what she called 'Special Favours', all kinds of wondrous activities which were horrendously expensive and all the more desirable because they were out of the reach of my pocket. Armed with the London street-guide we set off on the bus for Bayswater. I sat in a state of wistful dreaming, imagining the pleasures that lay ahead, but awakening to a distressing sense of my poverty. For the first time I felt desperate, a sudden hunger for money, a sudden terror of the emptiness of my pocket, the emptiness of my life. Shaz was right, everything was for sale. Troilus didn't spend enough. Otherwise he wouldn't have lost her. Kurtz should have come out with his boatload of ivory and paid for his sex instead of wanting it on the cheap with blacks who didn't know how much to charge because they didn't have a money system. He would have got turned on more if he paid for all the perversions, paid calmly and exactly, counting out the banknotes carefully after he had zipped up his trousers.

She was waiting at the doorway and surprised us, as we walked up the street checking the house numbers, by stepping out and asking in a loud Italian accent, 'Are you boys calling upon me tonight?' She was holding a white poodle which leapt out of her arms and barked about our feet. Shaz was busy avoiding the dog but I noticed immediately the exposed curves of her chest and the way her nipples pressed against her dress. She must have heard my beating heart for she asked me in a lowered, pleasing voice whether I was the one and her face lit up in a seductive smile, as if out of the two of us, she was charmed by *my* presence and would oblige any favour if only I would quickly step inside. I mumbled something and nodded Shaz's way to indicate that he was the one. Her eyes turned to Shaz, the smile still glued on her mouth, and I felt momentarily betrayed at her easy transference of affection. Shaz hesitated and returned the nod in my direction, identifying me as the sinner. I looked at him, puzzled, but his eyes were lowered to the ground, a film of guilt on his face as if he had betrayed me by handing me over to her. He focused on beating off the dog, which, sensing our timidity, was not only barking louder but baring its tiny teeth, whilst I slipped my hand into my empty pocket to cover up an overwhelming sense of nakedness. We lingered in this state of helplessness for some seconds before she suddenly shed her smile like a ton of armour-plating and growled, 'Come on, who's got the money then?' Shaz's hand jerked to his pocket in a reflex action, pulling out a ten-pound note; he stood there holding it up like a little contrite boy. In an agile pincer movement her fingers closed over the note, seized it and dropped it into her bosom, like the robot hand at Battersea Fun Fair which, when activated by a shilling, hovered over an array of gifts then descended swiftly, claws open, to pluck one up and deliver to its master. Nine out of ten times it seized upon nothing, the slippery plastic wrap of the packet of cigarettes or box of chocolates defeating its greed. She was no silly robot though. The money in her possession, she turned towards the house and Shaz and I followed her indoors on mechanical feet. 'She's a bit battered,' Shaz whispered when she disappeared into a bedroom and left us waiting in the corridor. 'Too old . . . you go in and have her . . . you can have it on me. Don't worry about the money.'

'She did warn you,' I replied, nudging him towards the room, 'I'll wait here, it'll be alright.'

'It's free man, go for it,' he urged below his breath, 'I can have it off with Monica whenever I like. You've not done Janet yet have you? You'll learn something from this old lady, honest, you'll be glad for the expertise. Italians know it all.' We lingered before the door, haggling, until a voice boomed out, 'Come in boys, it's warmer in here,' and we obeyed immediately, shuffling into the room. She had taken off her dress. She loomed large before us, breasts half-exposed and sagging from a cotton vest, and hips swelling out of red French knickers. I noticed a mole just above her navel. So long as I didn't look at her creased face I could easily lose myself in her body and handle it in delicious ways. A feeling of sturdiness overcame me, a new thrilling sense of adultness and resolve. I knew then I could do it, I had complete faith in myself, but this new courage from unknown sources waned as swiftly as it had arisen, for before I could take Shaz up on his offer he was already being led by the hand into an adjoining room.

I waited on the sofa, accusing myself of stupidity and straining to catch any sound coming from the bedroom. There was nothing, not even the creak of a bed. I contemplated peeping through the keyhole but the imagining of Shaz's naked body put me off. In our years of friendship we had never seen each other without clothes. That would have spoiled our relationship I felt sure, even though I could not explain to myself how and why, apart from a recollection, which I immediately made fuzzy, of Peter and I lying beside each other in the bushes behind my grandmother's house, our pants loose at our ankles. Nakedness was for a man and woman, not for boys like ourselves. I sat on the sofa feeling small and unformed and misplaced in this Bayswater room where men came and went, knowing what words to say, what actions to perform and spending money that only adults could possess. Better for me to stick to the books, better to learn to read the world through novels and that way prepare for the bigness of life until such time that I had to live it. Minutes passed; the poodle which was now seated neatly on the floor stared at me with intense curiosity and I stared back. It must have seen hundreds of us in its lifetime, each one different and each one the same. Only its mistress was recognisable among all the faces and smells. From the bedroom a tiny groan, more a squeak, interrupted my thoughts, and shortly after Shaz emerged grinning. Two days later on the bus to Westminster Hospital he described it.

She lay on the bed, called him over, unzipped his trousers and took it in her hands, rubbing it until it was stiff, then unpeeling a condom she daubed it in vaseline and rolled it over the stiffness. She adjusted her body to a comfortable position, and guided it into her. The sudden thrill made his mouth fasten upon her nipple childishly whilst she moved up and down. She whispered Italian words into his ears, with bits of English interspersed, like 'You're a strong, young thing,' and 'I bet you get all the girls going like this.' I imagined him wound to a peak of frenzy and flattery, closing his eyes and letting go, as Joseph had preached, falling and falling and not caring where he landed, just feeling the abandonment of weightlessness, while she gripped her muscles, trying to hold him back, to prevent him from falling and dissolving into air. The sex was so tingling he gave her an extra five pounds afterwards and promised to come back for more. She rubbed her tongue along her lips as if promising extra delights and manoeuvres next time.

'Did she come?' I asked, wanting to know what 'coming' for a woman meant.

'Sure,' he replied.

'How can you tell?' I persisted.

'You can see from their eyes: weak-looking and blank, you know.' I didn't know but I nodded anyway, all the same dubious of Shaz's confidence. According to the magazines there was a lot of noise and tearing of flesh when that moment came, and I had heard nothing as I waited apart from the feeble groan which could easily have come from the throat of the poodle for all I could remember. 'Plus she said so afterwards,' he added, lighting up at the memory of it, 'she thought I was a good lover, and she should know.' Suddenly, her age, which had so repelled him and caused us to hover at her door, was now a virtue. 'She should know,' he repeated, convincing himself of his prowess.

'So how did you get V.D.?' I asked, as we emerged from the clinic. The prescription protruded from the top pocket of his blazer like a snappy handkerchief.

'The vaseline, it must have had germs according to the doctor.'

I had waited in the company of guilty-looking men, hiding my face in a magazine, embarrassed that they might have thought that I too was diseased. Other men lit up cigarettes, hiding behind individual clouds of smoke. Shaz kept talking loudly to me, or flicking the pages of his magazine in an exaggerated manner, for he was not in the least ashamed. It was a mark of adventurous manhood and he wanted to show off the fact that he had slept with a whore and caught the necessary infection. 'Penicillin, I think,' he said boldly to the female chemist, smiling and handing over his paper. When she gave him the bottle of tablets he signed the prescription zestfully and put an 'x' after his name as if it were a love letter.

On our way to visit Joseph he made me swear not to tell Monica. 'She wouldn't care would she?' I asked, 'she's probably caught it already from some man.' He was hurt by my outspokenness and attempted to defend her integrity. 'She's not a common slut you know. She takes care of herself. Every week she goes for a check-up with her private doctor.' He fell silent for a while and I looked meekly to the ground in a gesture of apology. 'And don't tell Janet either, she wouldn't understand . . .' It was almost a plea, as if he wanted to engage her respect by protecting her from knowledge of his dirtiness. We walked along the street in embarrassed silence. 'She's the kind of girl for marrying,' he blurted out, 'you know, brought up in decency and all that.' His sudden warmth for her offended me in turn, but there was such a pang of regret in his voice that I felt sorry for him.

'You should stay on in school Shaz,' I said coaxingly, 'you've got the brains to get to university. All this sex stuff is a waste of time when you think about it.'

He wouldn't listen though, arguing that it was a business like any other. 'There's money in it. Sex is like food or water or clothes – everybody needs it and a lot of people will pay good money for it. Look at Patel.'

*   *   *

Pocket Patel had abandoned schooling just after obtaining his two 'O' levels to join what he called 'the enterprise culture'. 'Business is in our blood, man,' he said, 'and this country is wide open for everything.' He laughed with the confidence of a millionaire. 'You still reading all those books?' he asked in a voice of mock pity, 'how many "A" levels are you doing?'

'Three, and the Special Paper in English,' I confessed in a mixture of pride and embarrassment.

'Books finished you know,' he said, 'all people want are films,' and he gestured grandly in the direction of the shelves of video cassettes in his father's shop. 'Come behind the counter,' he urged, pulling me towards the till, 'and see what I see.' I stood behind the counter and looked out sheepishly. Patel moved away to talk to Shaz who was inspecting a poster. The films were arranged in separate rows, each neatly labelled. There was an 'Indian' section, a 'Western' one, and others marked 'Horror', 'Comedy', and 'Family'. I admired the way he had brought order to the hundreds of titles, so that a customer need not be bewildered but could wander around the shelves in complete ease. Standing behind the counter and looking through the shop and out to the world outside the window, cars moving past, children cycling on the pavement, shoppers bearing plastic bags, I understood Patel's confidence. The counter separated me from the mass of life outside the shop, it made me feel as solid and privileged as the polished oak it was made of. I was the proprietor, they were the anonymous public who needed me: coming in from the bustle and chaos to quietly browse through my goods, which were all laid out in a disciplined manner, each tagged with a correct number and price. When they left with the goods, the space in the wall filled me with sadness, as if I had lost something intimate, but calmness and happiness soon returned, for I knew the space would be filled before long by other items. 'Hello Mr Patel,' I imagined them saying, and I savoured the 'Mister', the token of respect, and the fact that I had a name which they knew, opinions and information which they sought. 'Any new videos in recently? Any good ones for children you can recommend? Have you got this one on Beta-Max? What's this one about? Which is the better thriller out of these two?' This is what it must be like to be an Asian shopkeeper, I thought, this sense of responsibility, power and control over the public, the way they looked respectfully at you behind the counter, depending upon you for your services.

In the few minutes before opening time I tried to convey all this to Patel. 'That's all foolishness,' he said, 'I don't give a damn for anybody as long as they pay. And if you think it's all smooth and orderly you should hang around here for a day. They come in and try to steal, if you don't keep a sharp eye on them you're done for. Or they bring back cassettes with the tape twisted or broken and argue how I've spoilt their machine and should pay compensation. When I try to reason with them they call me a Paki bastard and threaten violence. You see this here' – he pointed to a red button under the counter – 'that's wired straight to the police station in case of trouble.'

Shaz told me afterwards that Patel's business was doing so well that his father was opening up another shop in Tooting, with plans for a third outlet. 'It's all the sex films that he sells that brings in all the money. He's got them hidden under the counter, for special clients who pay ten pounds a time to borrow them.'

'Doesn't his father know?' I asked innocently.

'Of course you idiot. It's his father who flies over to New York and Amsterdam to put in orders. He goes there and watches dozens of them and makes a selection. When he can't go he sends Patel. They've got a system of smuggling the films into this country. It's all organised like a proper business.'

We turned into the street of abandoned houses where Joseph hid. As soon as I saw the decay I felt my feet hesitating, but Shaz strolled ahead nonchalant as ever. Nothing made sense. How was Patel, who only yesterday was running up and down the school corridors making a nuisance of himself, or lifting things from other boy's blazers, transformed into a pedlar of pornography? How could his father allow it? How could he send his son to watch all kinds of indecent films? And what about Patel's mother and three sisters? How could the father sell all that sex stuff which went against all their Indian beliefs? Indians were family people, everybody knew that. The men watched over the family, especially the girls whom they kept from dirt and who saved their virginities for marriage. For a moment I pictured Nasim's mother and the daughter Rashida, sitting before the television to watch men crawling over a naked woman, and the image so disgusted me that I banished it from my mind immediately. It was more proper to think of them watching Indian films, the kind I had grown up with in New Amsterdam, when my mother, in reward for some good deed in the house, like shining the windows, or sharpening all my sisters' school pencils, gave me the matinée money, and I grabbed it, shouted thanks and sped off to the Globe Cinema before she could call me back to perform some other task. Saturdays were Indian days, a double feature, but all the films were really the same story, all the songs sounded alike. A son leaves the village in search of work. His mother, a widow, falls upon him crying as he is about to go. His face is creased in sorrow, bravely he fights back the tears until he bursts into song, kneels before her, pays homage at her feet, promises to return soon with enough money to keep her through her old age. After a series of misfortunes in the city, when he is spurned or abused by the rich and powerful because of his lowly origin, he falls in love with a lawyer's daughter. One day he is pulling up weeds in their garden, his heart heavy with the memory of his mother, when he looks up and sees the daughter watching him from her bedroom window. She smiles shyly, and quickly but gracefully moves out of view, but he is transfixed, smitten by the glimpse of beauty such as he imagined his mother possessed when she was young. As he walks home to his hovel in the slum part of the city his soul trembles with strange emotions. Slowly he begins to sing, his steps quicken into a dance, other pedestrians also begin to dance with him, they form a chorus answering his questions about the nature of life, spurring him on to fulfil the destiny of his heart, and before long the whole neighbourhood is a throng of lights, a festival of music, women joining hands and skipping along the pavement, men swinging from lamp-posts, love lyrics pouring forth, even the street beggars tapping their sticks on the asphalt to keep up the rhythm, the song soon reaching a pitch of longing before winding down, the people slowly disappearing from view, the beggars taking up their sacks and walking away, and the son finally alone, as at the beginning, bleakness returning to the surroundings and his heart shrinking to the proportions of his poverty. After many episodes revealing setbacks, reversals, accidents, transformations and miracles, he eventually returns home with a suitcase of money, a motor car and his lovely bride, the lawyer's daughter, who had married him the day after he had qualified as a doctor. The mother, curled in a ball of distress on her mattress, coughing her lungs out, malnourished, looks up and sees them approaching. Her feeble eyes nevertheless recognise him, her heart skips, life returns to her limbs, with a mighty final heave she lifts herself up, reaches the door, opens it, stumbles into the yard to the gate. He, seeing her dying condition, switches off the motor, rushes out to her, catching her in time as she collapses in his arms. He kisses her frantically and her mouth responds, muttering a few words. He lays her down on the ground, resting her head on his jacket, and begins to sing, telling her of how miserable life was without her, how hard he had worked, how eventually he achieved his goal. Hearing of his success a smile creases her face for the first time in years, she breathes deeply, and dies. I am sitting on a bench in the darkness of the cinema clutching a parcel of peanuts, afraid to let go. I hear a few women behind me sobbing and the grief so unsettles me that the peanuts fall from my hand. I too feel like crying in the darkness, where no one can see me. I want to cry and cry like the son, and bury my face in her bosom and never stop crying. When I go home I am so glad to see my mother. I hide behind the star-apple tree in our yard and watch her hanging out the washing and sweeping the stairs. I see her hands moving nimbly and her feet scurrying here and there and everywhere. I know then that I must grow up soon so that I can earn lots of money and give her all. And I will marry Gildharry's daughter, Sita. She's black and ugly and a dunce and one day at school a louse fell from her head as she was bent over her spelling book and she squashed it, pop it went, and left a horrible red mark on the page, so that when I looked over I felt sick and fainted, and Miss Lambert our teacher called a big boy from a higher class who put me on his bicycle and took me home half-slumped over the handlebars. I hate Sita but Mr Gildharry has a big shop at the top of the road, the biggest in New Amsterdam, packed with all kinds of groceries and fancy things in tins, like sardines and peaches all the way from England, so that me and my mother and my sisters can eat all day and have everything we want.

*　　*　　*.

Joseph didn't bother to look up when we climbed over the hills of bricks and rubble and entered his retreat. He was squatting in the mud, staring at it in deep reflection as if he were an archaeologist plotting a dig, imagining hoards of priceless relics beneath the surface. He had a stick in his hand which he scraped periodically along the earth. We approached and Shaz hailed him. 'What's all this?' he asked, squinting at the marks Joseph had made in the mud, 'modern art or what?' I couldn't decipher the lines either. 'I get it,' Shaz said, 'it's a cave painting!' And he laughed cruelly. Joseph was unmoved. He continued scratching with his stick. Shaz was right as usual, though he had no cause to be so vicious, for when I studied Joseph in his dirt, shabbiness and torn clothing, he did look the very picture of a primitive mixing colours from crushed bone and blood to decorate his cave. I automatically handed over the plastic bag of food as if to placate his appetite and save our lives. He looked up, and I noticed a strange lethargy in his eyes, an abandonment of will, as if he had come to know everything and no longer wanted anything. 'Oh, it's you,' he said after a while, emerging from his sleep, and a light flickered in his eyes as if he were genuinely pleased to see me, 'I been waiting for you all day to come, what took you so long?' Before I could answer he reached into his back pocket and pulled out a scrap of newspaper. He scanned it, found what he was looking for, and pointed to it. 'What's that say, that word there?' I noticed how long his nails had grown, and how grained in dirt. 'That one there,' he repeated, jabbing at the word as I tried to read.

'Cocoon,' I said.

'Oh! Oh! that's what it is!' he exclaimed, a freshness and excitement returning to his face. He sighed with immense relief, pronouncing the word 'cocoon' over and over again as if it were a sacred ingredient in some mysterious ritual he was enacting in his mind. 'What it mean?' he asked, 'what?'

I was frightened by his insistence. 'It's like a womb,' I explained, 'a kind of warm place where eggs hatch and things are born.'

At this his whole appearance changed dramatically. He jerked into life. He was completely ecstatic, beside himself with glee, bolting upright and pacing up and down the floor of the slum. 'That's what I been writing all day, waiting for you to come and interpret,' he shouted out from the far corner of the room which was so devoid of light that he was completely invisible. He emerged from the gloom as suddenly as he had disappeared into it, grasped my hand and led me closer to the marks he had made in the mud. I peered hard at them, trying to make sense. They were the very first chaotic attempts he had made in his life to write something, apart from his name, the lettering of which he had memorised and practised until he could sign it legibly. 'It's me, all of that is me,' he explained, 'can't you see, can't you see,' a note of frustration in his voice as I tried my best to study the mud for clues to his identity. 'Here,' he said, 'here,' taking up the stick and pointing to the ground like a teacher before a blackboard, 'here is C and this one here is O and another C and two more O's, and then N.' I couldn't figure out what he meant, wondering if he had discovered a new cryptic way of signing his name, Joseph Countryman, by reducing it to a few random vowels and consonants. I thought he was being crazy as ever, seeing things with that curious illiteracy that made everything he uttered appear to be visionary, the product of genius. 'Look! C is half O,' he continued to jabber, 'it nearly there, but when it form O it breaking up again, never completing.' He grew wild at my incomprehension, snapping the stick in two and stabbing the pieces in the mud. 'A is for apple,' he babbled, 'B for bat, C is for cocoon, which is also coon, N is for nut, but it's really for nuts, N is for nothing, N is for nignog. Can't you see, all of it is me.'

I couldn't see, not for years, not until the solitary hours in Oxford University library trying to master the alien language of medieval alliterative poetry, the sentences wrenched and wrecked by strange consonants, refusing to be smooth and civilised, when Joseph returns to haunt me, and I begin to glimpse some meaning to his outburst. He stalks me even here, within the guarded walls of the library where entry is strictly forbidden to all but a select few, where centuries of tradition, breeding and inter-breeding conspire to keep people of his sort outside the doors. I am no longer an immigrant here, for I can decipher the texts, I have been exempted from the normal rules of lineage and privilege; yet he, an inveterate criminal, keeps breaking in to the most burglar-proof of institutions, reminding me of my dark shadow, drawing me back to my dark self. As my mind stumbles over the difficult words in *Sir Gawain*, I see a little boy's foot being trapped in the pits and cavities of hardened mud as he hurries after the sound of an old man's stick; I see Joseph's stick gouging letters in the mud, the sense of which now comes to me fitfully. He was telling me that he was half-formed, like the jelly in a cocoon, like the C trying to round itself to an O, getting there with great effort, but breaking up again because of the police, the Boys' Home, the absent father, the dead mother, the lack of education, the poverty, the condition of blackness. Even the quest for completion was absurd, for O signified nothing, the word ended with N for nothing. He was doomed to be a coon, like myself, like all of us, including those white Oxford students beside me bent over their books whom I glance at and feel stung by their brightness and confidence. They too are a waste of time. At least Joseph was humble enough to admit it.

I leave the library, climb onto my bicycle and pedal vaguely along the streets, not seeing the crowds of tourists entering and emerging from the quaint shops selling university souvenirs, expensive scarfs, silk ties, silver cutlery, specially labelled wines, hand-painted coats-of-arms. When the chain slips unexpectedly I dismount to fix it, my hands become covered in oil, and the shirt Janet bought me is smudged, and I know that Joseph is reminding me that he is still here, somewhere, that he has triumphed over all their greedy search for things, tokens, mementoes, status symbols. He stopped being a coon when he poured oil over himself and set light to the wick of himself, the flames letting me see how he was purifying himself of all the shame and desire by burning off his black skin, once and for all cracking and peeling it off, so that when the fire died there was mostly molten flesh, meat that could have been that of a white man, or an animal. Or perhaps he wanted to burn like a Hindu corpse to show us Asians that he was no different from us, that he was not an inferior being, that 'you is we', as Auntie Clarice had said.

When I get back to my college room, I wipe the oil away frantically and with clean hands I take up a pen and begin to write in the broken way that he spoke, in the broken way of the medieval verse, paying no attention to sense or grammar, just letting the words shudder out and form themselves. I am spellbound by his memory, I write in a fit of savagery, marking the page like stripes. I think of the agitation of his mind as he emptied the can of oil over himself, shaking the last drop out, as I now rattle and shake my mind for expression. Afterwards I am exhausted; I sprawl on the chair and when I look at what I have written I am utterly depressed. It is a mess of words, a mere illusion of truth. Joseph would have done it better. His confusions held some meaning. I suddenly long to be white, to be calm, to write with grace and clarity, to make words which have status, to shape them into the craftsmanship of English china, coaches, period furniture, harpsichords, wigs, English anything, for whatever they put their hands and minds to worked wonderfully. Everything they produced was fine and lasted for ever. We are mud, they the chiselled stone of Oxford that has survived centuries and will always be here. I sit in the library awed by the thousands of leather-bound volumes, some as old as recorded time, all carefully kept, lovingly restored by skilled hands and protected behind glass cabinets from soiling and vandalism and the gaze of the ignorant. I begin to despise Joseph, his babbling, his half-formed being, his lack of privilege, his stupid way of living and dying. I will grow strong in this library, this cocoon, I will absorb its nutrients of quiet scholarship, I will emerge from it and be somebody, some recognisable shape, not a lump of aborted, anonymous flesh.

'We have to help him, to save him like,' Shaz said as we left, 'he's going even more mad than he was.' His hands were plunged in his pocket, feeling the pound notes. I heard them rustling, and knew before he had need to explain that the solution involved some devious endeavour on Shaz's part. He would have a word with Patel, who was thinking of expanding his video business into film production to maximise profits. A business plan had been drawn up and all the calculations done. Shaz would procure the girls, Monica's companions on the street, and their boyfriends, for a fee. Patel would fund the whole project, providing premises and equipment. Joseph would operate the camera. After a few dummy runs, and group analysis of the film – its angle shots, zoom-ins, colour quality and the like – Shaz felt sure that Joseph would be competent enough to master the genre. 'After all, it's only a pussy opening and filling up, he can't go far wrong if he tries,' Shaz chuckled. When they asked me to write the script I laughed out of embarrassment. 'Business is not a joke,' Patel admonished me, his face taking on a seriousness I had never seen before. I still treated him as an old school friend, a bit of a dunce but good all the same for a game of football during the lunch-break. I imagined that he would grow up and be a bus conductor or electrician, a cheerful grin always on his face as he went about his humble tasks. Now I was standing behind the counter, his counter, surrounded by hundreds of films that he owned. I was stunned by the complete reversal in his fortunes. 'You've got to be deadly serious in this life if you want to survive,' he said sternly, 'or else you might as well be as hungry and ignorant and unemployed as all those white people out there.' I glanced meekly at my feet, feeling the sting of his warning. 'As far as I'm concerned, it's a real world, and every white person I see is worth ten pounds or one hundred pounds to me. Walking banknotes. Their skin is pale and shiny like coins. This country is full of them and we can make millions. Because they're lazy, good-for-nothing, they live for their bellies, from day to day. They save up, but only to blow it out on holidays. Eat and drink and watch videos and play football. My father says if he had known earlier he wouldn't have waited for General Amin, he would have left Africa earlier to come here. Black people don't have a cent to their names, so it's hard to make a decent living from them.'

'That's only the white working class,' I countered, 'the rest of them are better than us Pakis. All we want to do is run shops and chew pan. At least they write books and all that.'

Patel became even more incensed, wounded by my insult to his profession and his people. 'Books!' he scoffed, 'a lot of fancy words on paper! You are just pretentious with all that book talk. All you want is to imitate the white people, because you are ashamed to be like me, ashamed that people will call you a Paki. But let me tell you, I'm a rich Paki, a happy Paki, and they have to come to my shop, and they wish it was their shop, they're full of envy, but they don't know how to run one properly, they don't like working, so they sell out to the first Paki who comes in with a chequebook and run across the road to the nearest pub.'

'Take it easy,' Shaz intervened, sensing a fist fight, 'everybody to their own thing, that's what I say,' pointing to a poster and ogling at the half-naked woman exaggeratedly to diffuse tensions. Patel calmed down, searched under the counter and pulled out a document marked 'Business Plan' in bold red type.

'Honest,' he said, his voice lowered in friendship, trying to make peace with me, 'people don't read books anymore, not even white people. It's all films nowadays,' and he gestured towards the cassettes in the shop. 'Look here, it's all here.'

I took the document from him in a gesture of reconciliation and read. It was a series of figures, which I could not understand, some laid out in neat rows like cassettes on his shelves, others plotted on a series of graphs.

'I bet you can't read that,' he said triumphantly, 'but that's the real book nowadays. Here, shall I teach you?' he mocked, and he made as if to take the papers from my hand and give me a lesson in the way that I once did as the 'professor'. Shaz smiled viciously, relishing my downfall. I looked at the words written down as headings or as introductions to the sums, 'Accrued Expenses', 'Historic Cost Convention', 'Nett Realisable Value', and the like, secretly admiring Patel's new erudition, remembering the boy whose only polysyllables were plucked out of the *Thesaurus* and memorised. No more tigers 'embellished' by the sun's rays or 'sepulchral' in the moonlight. His business plan banished all wildness, removed the animal claw and fang, replaced them with colourless, neutral integers, yet I knew instinctively that the latter were more dangerous, that the sums and figures were more threatening, that they could lock you away in prison for the rest of your life, or give you power to crush heads, obtain whatever or whoever you wanted or willed, the most beautiful and inaccessible of women falling greedily upon your lap, the gold in their teeth flashing as they opened their mouths. I looked up at the poster that Shaz was still admiring with a pang of attraction and regret.

I was bent over blank pages when Janet rattled at the door and came in. I didn't want to see her and she picked up my mood instantly. After a brief greeting she made herself at home, putting the kettle on the stove and rinsing a cup. I went back to the essay, not knowing what to say to her. 'Miserable as usual,' she said, plonking the coffee before me, clanking the spoon in and stirring it. She seemed to spill a few drops deliberately onto the page and I wiped them away with irritation. 'When you screw up your face like that you lose all the handsomeness,' she continued, her flattery eliciting an involuntary smile from me. 'Ever since I've known you, you're nothing but worried. Either brooding about the past, or plotting for the future, never here in the present, relaxed.'

'I can't live like white people,' I retaliated, quoting Patel, 'I can't think only of today and to hell with everything else.' I waited for an argument to develop, but she refused to be drawn, continuing in her blithe way to advise me to take things easy. She sat on the bed sipping her coffee and staring into the mug. She rubbed her tongue occasionally along her lips and when she lowered her head her hair fell about her face, disguising it. Patel's talk of sex and of white women doing it gladly for money emboldened me. I wanted her. She must have heard my thoughts for she looked up and stared at me with knowing eyes, a shy smile on her face. I heard Mr Ali coughing with grief downstairs. He was still missing his sister and would walk up and down the staircase, often coming unannounced into my room for an idle chat. There was no lock on the door, Janet and I would have to be quick, in case he stirred, wandered upstairs and surprised us. If I had money I would have taken her to a hotel far away from this slum town, to a spacious room with large sunlit windows overlooking woods. There would be a deep bed, fresh linen, the room would contain all manner of attractive fittings, bedside lamps, intriguing pictures on the wall, a remote control television and a refrigerator stocked with miniature bottles and sandwiches. But I knew that even with money I would lack courage to walk past the uniformed doormen and push through the swing doors, never mind stand before the plush counter and enquire whether a double room was vacant. Janet would hide behind me and shrivel with shame. We were too young for such a rendezvous and I lacked the necessary confidence, colour and polished appearance to pass for a scion of privilege and teenage promiscuity. She was doomed to my single bed with its stained pillow and ravelled blanket.

I drew the curtains to hide my fear, moved towards her and lowered her to the bed, utterly surprised when her body surrendered to the pressure of my hands and lay passively horizontal. As I fumbled to undo my trousers she slipped off her skirt and held me close to her, pressing my face to her neck and breasts. I eased her panties down to her ankles. Everything was proceeding so smoothly that I was already filled with a sense of manly accomplishment: my heart stopped beating wildly and a strange calm seized me, as if such love-making had always been within my capacity. The fear surged back as suddenly as it had disappeared when I tried to push my stiffness into her and found the hole unmanageably small. I paused, then pushed again, but nothing gave, no sudden opening, no delicious force sucking me in, no delirium of the mind, no gasping as the books had suggested. I tried again and again, in the brief intervals delving my hand beneath her blouse and feeling her breasts, but in a mechanical way, desperate attempts to keep her aroused. The pleasure of the whole act had long since drained for me, I kept going only out of stubborn pride. I imagined Joseph perched over us, his camera rolling, with Patel seated in my chair, like a director, a megaphone held to his mouth, and I felt myself drooping. I wondered what Patel meant when he asked me to write the scripts. I could think of nothing but 'ooohs' and 'aaahs'. Patel had said he was hoping to provide Punjabi subtitles, so that he could develop a market in India, and now, perched over Janet, I found myself wondering how 'ooohs' and 'aaahs' sounded in Punjabi. The same surely? The lettering would be different of course, but surely the Indians were not so daft that they needed to read the sounds uttered in delirium. Thankfully Mr Ali slammed the door downstairs, I froze in mock fright, leapt up and pulled up my trousers, relieved that it was all over.

I boiled the kettle and made us a cup of tea, hoping that Mr Ali would burst into the room at any moment and so salvage my credibility. I turned my back to her to give her privacy to rearrange her clothes. We sat silently, nibbling on biscuits.

'When are you going for your interview?' she said, looking up at me and smiling in forgiveness at my uselessness.

'Two weeks on Thursday.' I was relieved that a conversation could be started up. She enquired how I
would get to Oxford, and I said by train.

'I am going through that . . . what poetry is all about
. . . in case they ask,' I said as she picked up Shelley's
Apology for Poetry and flicked through it.

'Well, what's it all about? Pretend I'm the board of
scholars and you are sitting before me.' She sat upright,
brushed her hair back as if getting into the role. 'Start
apologising.'

'It's like a seed, according to Shelley, containing the
past and the future plant,' I said as impressively as I
could, but knowing that it sounded foolish and pretentious.

She picked up on my embarrassment. 'Well, I sup-
pose it depends on what kind of plant – either a sissy
daffodil or a Venus fly-trap. I bet Shelley was thinking of
daffodils. Men always go for vulnerable images, things
they can control and dominate. Me, I think poetry is
a meat-eating, cunning flower that traps your tongue
and never lets go.' And she laughed, rose from the
bed, put down her cup and moved to the door. 'Well,
do your best in Oxford and make sure you get in this
time.' She burst into a smile, winked at me and left.

IV

I WAIT FOR THE TAXI to arrive, early in the morning. 'It will take at least three hours,' they said, 'make sure you're ready to go as soon as the car comes, to miss the rush hour. Otherwise you will have to pay more.' I am excited and nervous as I wait among my belongings at the front of the house. Everything is packed into a suitcase and four cardboard boxes which the Asian whom I used to steal from supplied from the back of his shop.

'I want to arrive in style, so don't give me any tatty boxes.'

He brought out about six or seven. Right away I rejected the ones with garish letters proclaiming their contents of soap powder or tomato soup. I didn't want anybody in Oxford associating me with the lettering of corner-shop trade. I imagined unpacking my clothing, lining up my books on the shelves with a sense of achievement, feeling proud at the new surroundings, the clean college room with scrubbed stone walls, my home at last, but afterwards realising in a flash of panic that there were four empty Heinz or Surf boxes looming on the floor, diminishing the scholarly ambience of my room by reminding me of my indefinite past. I will die with embarrassment having to take the four boxes along the corridor, down the stairs, into the sunshine illuminating the quad, towards the porter's lodge for disposal, always under the direct gaze or sly glance of my fellow students. Perhaps I will leave them on the floor, and they will go away by themselves. Or I will break them up, and when night comes I will take them in one anonymous bundle to the bins, where my life, up to this moment, belongs.

Everything is neatly arranged at my feet. The boxes are securely tied up, the suitcase locked. I feel in my left blazer pocket for the umpteenth time to make sure the key is there, always forgetting that it is in the right-hand pocket and panicking for a moment when I cannot find it. I think of Patel as my fingers discover the key, fearful that he is around somewhere in the semi-darkness, switching things from one pocket to the next to create the maximum disorientation of my mind. I have two other pockets, one containing the thirty-pound fare, the other fifty pounds, in case lavish entertainment was expected in the first week – dinner in restaurants, sherry and so on. Each sum is in a separate pocket to avoid confusion. I am ready and waiting. Perhaps I should have saved the money and taken the train as the Asian shopkeeper had recommended. It's too late now.

'Thirty pounds!' he exclaimed as I told him, and swore in Punjabi, 'that is lot of money. You mad? Why you not take train?'

But I wanted to arrive with a dignity befitting the place, not with plastic bags and a social worker as at the Boy's Home. I was sure too that most of the students would be chauffeured there by their parents, and I didn't want to be the odd one out at the very beginning. Another summer's engagement at Battersea Fun Fair, and especially the unofficial wages got by cheating, had given me enough money to fill my suitcase with brand new clothing. Shaz had given me one hundred pounds in cash, which I took guiltily, wondering whether he knew about me and Monica, but he shoved the notes in my pocket and told me to shut up when I began to mumble my thanks, and that I didn't even have to write, he'd still send a small piece every month, so long as I kept passing the exams and whipping them white boys' arse with bright essays and giving all them aristocratic girls one nightlong one for him, who talk so posh as if they suck cock-pebbles in their mouths. I knew this parting obscenity was really to mask his sadness at my going, for he dug his hands into his pocket and felt about forlornly as if wanting to find more money and hand it over to me.

'And I don't want to see you back here until term-end. Don't start getting frighten and run back,' he said sternly, adopting the role of a big brother. He knew though that I would never return, neither during term-time nor during the vacations. And if I did I would be a different person, a new accent in my voice, bigger words for bigger ideas, all of which would be beyond him. Like Nasim's mother he didn't want me to ever come back to Balham. I had called in to say goodbye. Rashida answered the door. She looked at me shyly, not knowing what to do. I glanced down at the mat and enquired whether Mrs Khan was at home. She opened the door and let me in without speaking. I followed her down the darkened corridor, knowing that if I touched her she would succumb, and into the sitting-room where Nasim's mother sat knitting. I wished Rashida was at home by herself as at our first meeting, for I felt sure I could talk to her now, though I couldn't think about what. She seemed so different from when I had last visited, about two years previously, the childishness lost from her body, and replaced by odd curves and swellings. Even her hair, which was once long and flowing, was now shorter, giving her face a more eager appearance. Mrs Khan looked up from her balls of black wool, saw me and stretched out her arms in welcome. I kissed her on the cheek, guilty that I was lusting after her daughter. It would have been a betrayal to have tampered with her, not so much of Nasim and his mother, but of my own feelings about the need for family. It would have been like sleeping with a sister. Janet and Monica, yes, but not an Asian girl like Rashida who looked so vulnerable. The whole sitting-room, so green and alien, green sofas, green map on the wall, the colour of Pakistan, the Eastern vases, the model of the Kaaba, the sticks of incense, the brown dolls, they were all vulnerable to being smashed up, vulgarised. I knew that we had to look after each other, that I could not copulate with her in the free manner of Patel's film-stars.

Nasim was still in Sheffield, working in a bank, and staying with his uncle and aunt. I asked after him in a perfunctory manner, for he had long ceased being a close friend, and I had not seen him since he failed most of his 'O' levels and left school. 'Write,' I had said to him, knowing that he wouldn't, that the shame of his bruises would forever alienate him from us. I was glad to know that he was employed in the safest of settings, behind a counter protected by a glass grille and burglar alarms.

Mrs Khan was overjoyed that I was about to leave for Oxford, as if I had fulfilled all the trust she had placed in me.

'Any mother proud to have you as son,' she beamed in her broken English, and waved Rashida to the kitchen to prepare some food.

I nodded, and said nothing. She looked at me compassionately, as if knowing what had been uppermost in my mind as soon as the formal letter had arrived offering me a place at the university. It coincided with a haphazard one from my mother, telling me, in a struggling English, the verb-tenses mixed up so that I couldn't figure past from present from future, how my eldest sister, Droopatie, soon to marry, and Seta train to be nurse, the boy Raj is from decent family, his father does run a small cake-shop in Pitt Street and they go move to a small house in Nelson Road, just outside New Amsterdam, when wedding day done. The white people's names on our streets suddenly stand out and make no sense. And my sisters are strangers, I don't know them. I have forgotten what my mother looks like. There are no clever cameras in the place to fix time. It has been six years or more. I hold both letters in my hand and stare into the mirror, wondering how I have changed, whether they would recognise me if I suddenly appeared in New Amsterdam, rattled the gate and called out in my English voice. I look again at my mother's letter, trying to read the handwriting, the twist and curl of letters, for clues to her appearance, before realising that it was probably written by one of my sisters, or by the neighbour, since she couldn't write, or at least I can't remember her ever writing. I dredge my mind trying to recall if I ever saw her with a pen in her hand, but everything is blank. All I can remember is the tall star-apple tree in the front yard which I climbed up every afternoon when it was bearing, slipping and scratching my legs and nearly falling off, but too hungry for its sweet fruit to bother with my safety. She stood with a stick in her hand, waving it and threatening me if I didn't come down that minute. There was the carilla vine at the side of the house which she tended, picking them for the pot, together with bora and tomato. In the backyard was our fowl-pen. I can recall her with grains of rice in her hand, flinging them at the hens, or carrying bunches of vegetables indoors, or a broom which she gripped and swept the steps and the floor with, always sweeping, sweeping, even when no dust was in sight. But I cannot picture her with a pen in her hand. My father had one in his top pocket, a fat brown one with a clip. He was always writing on pieces of paper, looking so serious that we were afraid to go near him in case we disturbed him. I sit quietly playing with my mother's cotton reels or with buttons, listening to his pen scratching the paper like a fat cockroach crawling along the wooden floor. I am glad he is so concentrated on his pen because then he will not think to hit her. When I grow up I will stab him with the nib of his pen if he raises his hand to her. I will stamp on him and squash him as he tries to scurry under the furniture. My mother scrubs the pocket of his shirt to get the ink-stain out, because the pen leaks. The shirt must always be crisp and white or he'll get vexed and start shouting at all of us.

She blessed me before I left the house, took my face in her hands and kissed me on both cheeks. She slipped some money into my blazer pocket, and gave me food, two tins of cooked meat curry and boiled channa, to take to Oxford. She ordered Rashida to wrap up half a dozen chapatis in tin foil, and all the samosas she could find in the fridge. Not satisfied she had given me enough, she looked about the room, alighted on a few books on the sideboard, took one up and handed it to me. It was the Koran, an English translation. I feigned gratitude, took up my presents and left. When I was far from the house I threw away all the food, not wanting my Oxford room to smell with curry and spices, but I kept the book, because a book is valuable and dignified. I felt bad as the food plopped into the bottom of the bin. For a moment I thought of retrieving it. I remembered how my grandfather cruelly drank all of Auntie Clarice's five-dollar note in the rum shop with his hooligan friends, the day before I left Guyana for England.

I shift from foot to foot, impatient for the car's arrival and feeling the keenness of an early-morning breeze. I don't know anybody anymore, it's as if I have already arrived at college and put an unbridgeable distance between us. I've only known them on the surface, Shaz and Joseph. Now and again they would say and do something which would reveal some aspect of their character. But in the end all you're left with is a random collection of memories which you try to piece together into some grander truth. As to Patel, he appeared in my life, then vanished as mysteriously as the things he switched from pocket to pocket. He never returned to school at the end of one summer's vacation, and I never bothered to enquire after him in any detail, partly because I became engrossed in my work, partly because I knew he was an immigrant, like myself, liable to disappear as suddenly as he had materialised. Now he was a shopkeeper, a trader, a professional rather than a person, someone whom I could not recognise as a childhood friend.

Perhaps I'm not old enough, or well-read enough, to know anything deeply. Perhaps I am not English enough: a piece of pidgin, not knowing where the past ended, where the present began, not knowing how the future was to be made. The years at Oxford would see to that though. Perhaps I will return to them after a long period of study, and then I will be able to talk properly with them, knowing who they are, who I am. But what would I say to Monica? I had nothing to tell her a week ago when she let me take her and afterwards I lay on my back on the grass in Tooting Bec Common, blinking involuntarily at the millions of stars which were so close that they were almost like flecks of glass in the film of my eyes and I could have reached for the moon and popped it into my mouth like a mint. I didn't want to speak, I just lay there and listened to my own breathing until it died down and became inaudible.

'Shaz wants to meet you in the Mariner's Arms,' she said, as I opened the door.

I was surprised at her being there, since she had never before visited my room.

'He sent me to fetch you,' she explained, 'He's doing some business with Patel and he'll join us later. It's important.'

We walked to the pub mostly in silence. I was reluctant to go since I would have preferred meeting in a less public, noisy, smoke-filled place.

'I hear you're off to university soon,' she said.

'Next week,' I answered bluntly.

'You're so clever,' she enthused, the suddenness of her admiration catching me by surprise, 'Everybody is glad for you; me too.'

I looked at her and smiled, not knowing what to say.

'I'd like to go to university,' she said after a while and waited for my response.

'Why don't you, you've got enough brains to get there.'

'Honest, you think so, really?' She seemed so grateful for my kind opinion.

'Yes, I do,' I lied, my eyes catching her large breasts flopping up and down as she walked in her high heels. The whoring had so developed her body that it seemed more adult than mine. I felt bony and awkward and spotty beside her.

'I wouldn't go though. I hate my father. He's so clever and smarmy. I hate him. He was at university.' She unwrapped a piece of gum, put it in her mouth and chewed loudly as if to assert her vulgarity, her resolve never to belong to a precious world of education and middle-class virtues.

We waited in the pub until closing time but Shaz did not show up. There was nothing to do but get drunk with the rest of the crowd since I could not prolong any conversation with Monica, and in any case I was fed up with the way men at the adjoining tables kept ogling at her body. Whenever she went to the bar it took her fifteen minutes to return with the drinks, someone or other chatting her up and offering to buy her whatever she wanted. I sat gloomily, puffing on a cigarette, watching her throw back her head and laugh or else twirl her forefinger round her hair coquettishly as she listened to them. When she came back and sat down, her short skirt pulled up revealing even more flesh, and there was a lull in the surrounding conversation, all eyes seemed drawn to the darkness between her thighs, dreaming of its fragrance and warmth. From where I sat, if I slumped low into the chair, I could see that she wore red panties, and as I got steadily more drunk I began to surrender to the general fantasy. I felt superior to the other men because I could see up her skirt, and the privileged perspective satisfied my ego. I spread out my legs and stared under the table in an attitude of lethargy, but secretly glancing at her legs, catching the colour of her panties whenever she shifted. She kept opening her thighs and closing them again, picking up the beer mat and fanning herself, as if the heat was irritating her body, all the time looking at me and smiling. We spoke a few words before sips, nothing in particular. She insisted on buying all the drinks, saying that she was treating me before I left for Oxford. By the time the pub closed we had drunk at least two bottles of cheap wine between us. It was only as I rose to go that I remembered that Shaz had not turned up and that I had not bothered to express puzzlement or anxiety about his absence.

We walked home across the Common, both swaying from the alcohol. I held her hand and arm now and again, as if to steady her. When we reached the middle, she said her new shoes were chafing at the ankle, and could we stop while she put on a plaster. We sat on the grass. She fumbled in her bag for a plaster, found one, but her fingers were too unsteady to peel off the wrapper. I took it from her, she kicked off her high heels and stretched her foot in my direction, curving it tantalisingly, her toes brushing playfully against my chest. She lay back and pulled me towards her. I was surprised at how utterly composed I was. The alcohol gave me total control of my nerves and body so that my hands were graceful as they played with her. She 'writhed and moaned' like the women in the magazine letters, but I was calm and masterly, entering her body effortlessly. The only disruption came when I ceased feeling anything for a moment and I wondered whether I had slipped out and was merely fencing about in air. I put my hands at the lip of the opening and was relieved to find that I was securely inserted. The sense of pleasure flooded back, but the temporary loss of sensation made me panic; I gripped her closer, closed my eyes tightly, determined to finish before anything went wrong so that I could at last feel that I had done it with a woman, broken my duck and scored an opening single as Shaz would have put it. His sexual language changed daily, depending on whatever took his fancy. If he visited as I was frying chips or sausages for instance, the talk would be about pricking, foreskin, tomato sauce likened to menstrual blood, and so on. Recently, Pakistan was playing test cricket against England and he would come to my room and watch an hour of it on television, grow bored and invent all kinds of rhymes and jingles as the batsmen flashed or the ball scooted along the grass to the boundary, like 'have a fuck and break your duck,' 'a quick single makes you tingle,' 'hit a four with the sweetest whore.'

'You're not the only poet in Balham,' he would say, 'I hope you're taking all this in, and when they ask you at Oxford where you learnt how to write, tell them the truth.' He cackled, gulped down his beer, compressed the empty can, aimed at the bin across the room, threw it in and applauded as if he had clean bowled England's best batsman. I looked at him wondering whether he would ever grow up.

I awoke not knowing how I had got to bed, then remembered the sex with Monica, unsure as to whether I had dreamt it. My body felt bruised and sticky, and when I examined myself in the mirror I was vaguely excited to see the traces of teethmarks. I wondered whether I had ejaculated in her. The stickiness suggested so, but then again it was not conclusive evidence. It suddenly struck me that Monica was Shaz's parting gift to me, his way of bolstering my self-confidence so that I could take on the intellectual challenge of Oxford.

'You have a head-start boy,' I could imagine him roaring with laughter, 'they're a bunch of wankers up there, they wouldn't know a girl's armpit from her fanny.' I was filled with gratitude, and suddenly knew how deep his friendship was, and his true nature.

I sat on the bed, naked, straining to recall the sensations of Monica's body. They returned in tantalising fragments and I savoured each one. If Janet had been there I felt sure I could have done it this time. I looked at the table of books and began to share Patel's contempt for them, wondering whether I had the courage to team up with him and spend the rest of my life in a haze of alcoholic sex.

My body was aroused by the thought, but I opened my eyes immediately, startled by footsteps outside the room. For a moment I thought it was my grandmother coming to catch me as she did when Peter and I ventured into the bush to play with ourselves. My cousin had come to board with us in New Amsterdam, having secured a job as a salesman in the Bata shoe-shop. It was he who had taught me to do it. We were bathing under the shower and when I washed away the soap and looked up I saw his penis fat and stretched and black as a donkey's. There were a pair of wild donkeys outside our school compound. Normally they grazed quietly between the trees, ignoring us as we played in the schoolyard – even when we pelted them with stones which merely bounced off their bodies. After a while we gave up trying to harass them, discovering some other means of mischief. One day we heard a hideous braying coming from the trees, and when we dropped our cricket bats and ran up to investigate, we were amazed at the sight of one donkey half on the back of the other, trying to push a monstrous black pole of flesh into it. The girls stood giggling or staring with mouths open, but we took up stones and hurled them at the donkeys. The one on top remained unmoved, even though a big stone struck it right between its eyes. It was so maddened with desire that nothing mattered but the stiffness and positioning of the pole. The other donkey seemed to shift away but was held back by the grip of its partner's hooves. It brayed in pain, or at least the horrible noise it made didn't suggest it was having fun, yet it stood its ground as the other drove into it. The pole glistened with slime, some of which dripped in blobs on the grass. The bell rang and we reluctantly abandoned them to return to classes. When we hurried back at the end of the school day, we found the two donkeys munching idly and peacefully, as if nothing unusual had happened. They looked up at us for a moment, then casually went back to their grazing.

He looked down and laughed at me staring at his thing. He showed me how to get my own one stiff. All I had to do was to rub it up and down, and close my eyes. He watched me doing it, stooping down to correct the position of my fingers when I got it wrong, then standing back to inspect the correctness of my procedure. After a while a sharp sensation ran through my body and made me shiver, as if the water from the shower had suddenly turned icy cold. The feeling lasted for no more than a second but left me dizzy. My cousin helped me out of the shower, steadying me by the elbow, whispering to me not to tell anything to my mother. Every afternoon we bathed together. We stood at opposite ends of the shower, closed our eyes and rubbed ourselves until the sensation came from nowhere and left us breathless. I always finished first, then stood and watched him doing it. He had a bigger pole because he was older. I wondered whether my one would swell to his size and leak whiteness when I grew up. Every day I went to school I looked at the two donkeys with awe. I no longer had a desire to throw stones at them.

'You ever pump?' I asked Peter when the holidays

came and I found myself in Albion Village, knowing that he was too much of an ignorant country boy to know what pumping was. He looked at me dumbly, before stammering something about cricket, asking me whether it was like a leg-break or a bouncer. I laughed contemptuously and led him through the bush behind my grandmother's house to a safe spot where I slipped off my pants. He watched, fascinated by my action, and fumbled to undo his own. I closed my eyes, overcome by the shiver of sensation. When I opened my eyes he was still sitting on the ground, rubbing away clumsily, with no effect. I was puzzled, and instructed him to close his eyes and try again, try hard. He closed his eyes, screwed up his face and shook away vigorously. I urged him on.

'Can you feel anything?' I asked, and he stammered that he didn't know.

My grandmother came upon this scene of debauchery, but I was concentrating too hard on Peter's body, giving him directions, to hear her approach. In shock, she dropped her bag of mangoes; they rolled everywhere. Peter automatically went to pick them up for her, but tripped over his trousers which were still loose around his ankles. He fell on his face, his fat brown buttocks quaking in the air. My grandmother hauled me up, took me by the hair and led me home, and as I cried all the way there she threatened to put me on the next bus to New Amsterdam. I blamed Peter, saying it was his idea, but she threatened to pour a gallon of castor oil down my throat to clean up all the lies.

This was the second time she had caught me, and

there was the same feeling of shame. I didn't understand what it was, and why I felt it, but as she dragged me along I knew that I had done something horrible and wrong. The first time she came upon me, I was staring at the body of the doll. She took it away roughly and put it back in its box, ordering me to leave the bedroom and go downstairs to help my grandfather lock up the sheep. One of my uncles from the city had sent the doll to Albion Village as a gift for Peter's sister, after their father had been found at the bottom of the Canje River. He had been eaten up by fish. Whenever I saw Richilo cleaning fish I expected a human eye to pop out like a pearl from the belly. I stopped eating fish soon after. Only the hunger of England drove me to the tins of sardines from the Asian shop, and even then I ate reluctantly, feeding most of them to Janet.

There were scars on his face, and a sack of stones tied to his feet. No one could discover who killed him and why, but some people said that he did wickedness with a girl, and left her with child, and the brothers trapped and beat him and dumped him in the river. Albion Village was excited, the rum shop noisier than usual, the dominoes slammed down on the table with new vigour and Kumar's bus hooted the news from one village to the next.

The white cardboard box lay on my grandmother's bed. She was in the kitchen. I slipped into the bedroom when she was not looking, somehow knowing that I was not allowed to touch it in case I got it dirty. When the box arrived, she had opened it, and held up the doll. It had creamy white skin, smooth and strangely different from anything I had ever seen before, and a white cotton dress with tiny yellow flowers. It had short golden hair, curling prettily around the face, and pink lips. When my grandmother raised it up, the long eyelashes opened, and I felt weak as it looked at me with blue eyes. I wanted to hold it close to my body but my grandmother put it away in the box.

I raised the lid and peeped in to discover her sleeping, but with the same gentle smile on her face, the same pink glow on her cheeks, and I was sure that nothing else in this world was as lovely. I wiped the moisture from my hand onto my shirt and picked her up, holding her nervously by the waist. She opened her eyes, and out of fright and shame I hurried to put her back in the box before she had a chance to see how ragged I was compared to her in her rich dress; how dark-skinned and ugly, the sweat forming on my face in contrast to the cool, dry feel of her flesh. The scent of her dress and her body made me feel unclean. I gazed at her lying so forgivingly in her box, as if she was not disturbed in the slightest by my rough handling of her. I noticed the neat bow on her shoes, knowing that my cousin and the whole of the Bata shop could never sell anything so pretty. She was wearing white socks, and I was sorry for her, for in this heat her feet were bound to suffer, only rich people in the city wore socks though the sun hot-hot, and I wished Ma could send her back to England where she belonged, instead of trapping her here with all the coolie and nigger people who would manhandle her and drop her on the floor so she'd hurt her head, so crude and ignorant were they, or all the fat black flies would congregate around her, mosquito night-time would bite her skin. Why were our people so cruel to bring her to such nastiness? I took off her shoes and socks, marvelling at how tiny, how perfectly shaped and pink her toes were, not like Ma's all cracked and gnarled. The curves of her naked feet aroused me, I was drawn upwards to her thighs. I was overcome by an intense curiosity to peep under her dress. I raised it with trembling fingers and was paralysed at the sight of her. I stood there gazing upon her body, and I felt my fingers fumbling to pull down her white slip to discover what lay underneath. It was beautifully white and smooth, hairless, not like Ma's when she and I bathed together and I waited until her eyes were closed because she was pouring water over her head, then I watched her quickly, seeing how dark and hairy and withered she was, and I wondered how come my sisters' were so clean and smooth, whether they would grow up to become bushy and nasty-looking like a malabunta nest.

She boxed my ears, sent me downstairs, where I mooned among the sheep grazing in the yard, waiting to be driven into the pen. I hated the smell of sheep, they dropped black dung everywhere which oozed between my toes. Even when I washed my feet the smell remained. I hated the nastiness of the whole village. I hated my grandmother. Richilo was right to curse her, calling her a tar-baby, a low-caste, louse-ridden, yam-headed, dog-eared, hungry-belly, black-skinned, buck-toothed whore, more sour-mouthed than tamarind, more hard-hearted than turtle shell, more slimy than fish-guts, stinkier than latrine, more pissy than monsoon, more . . . he took one last swig of rum and running out of images collapsed on his rice-sack bed. I hid under the bed-sheet, trembling with fear yet aroused by his power of speech. I wished I could describe things like Richilo. When day broke, I went downstairs to watch my grandfather milking the cows. The milk in his bucket was the colour of the inside of a young guava. His fingers pulled at the cow's teats like crab-claws. The cow was as red as Ma's headscarf. It's feet were as skinny and crooked as Pa's stick. The stubble on his chin looked like Ma's pin-cushion. My belly groaned with hunger. I rubbed it and was surprised to find how round and smooth it was, like a calabash shell. I was confident that when I grew up I would be as clever as Richilo in seeing things and using words. I spent the whole day wandering about the yard in a state of vague excitement, inspecting everything: pebbles in the grass, the grass itself, the path that ran through the grass, ending at one end of the yard at a rickety gate made of coconut branches strapped together by rope, at the other, stairs leading up to the kitchen door, and I tried to compare everything to everything else. Sometimes it was easy. I knew exactly what Pa's fish net resembled for example. He took me to the pond in the backdam. The net was folded up like an umbrella. I stood back as he swung his arms and twirled his body towards the water, the net lifting and opening wide like a woman's skirt caught by a sudden breeze. Mostly it was difficult. I screwed up my forehead for at least half an hour trying to figure out what the cow's skull resembled. It was stuck on a pole in the middle of the vegetable garden, to scare the birds. I tip-toed to peer into the holes where its eyes were, but could see nothing, only bone white as the doll's skin. A few black ants were crawling about the place where its nose was. I stepped back to examine it. I walked around it. Nothing came. I stood before it, immersing myself in thought. The more I looked the more terrifying it became, so that when my grandmother approached from behind and hollered at me to get out of the hot sun or I'll catch illness and headache, I jumped with fright, imagining that the noise has come from its jaws. She was carrying a pail of dry cow-dung to spread around the flowers. I saw the bodies of a few dead flies encased in the dung, having drowned in it when it was fresh and liquid.

'Ma, how the skull look to you, what you think it be like?' I asked as she broke up the cow-dung and sprinkled it on the flower bed. The dry, black pieces lay strangely among the red and orange petals which glistened in the sunlight, swimming in their own sweat. She stared at me as if my head had been afflicted by sunstroke, then returned to her work. I felt hatred for her again. I wished she would tell me things when I asked. Not only was she dark-skinned, she was ignorant as well. I looked at the cow's skull, ugly and broken and scarred by the weather and time, its jaws set in silence, its eyes empty of feeling, suddenly knowing that it resembled the whole of Ma. I longed to see the doll again.

*   *   *

'Goodbye white man,' Patel said, as I called to tell him I was leaving for Oxford next week. He was putting up a new poster advertising some trashy film, 'Night Angel', or some such title. It displayed a beautiful woman lying on white satin sheets, her clothes dishevelled from a struggle or else in eager preparation for one. It was difficult to tell whether the look on her face was one of alarm or anticipation. A man loomed over her, his shadow darkening the whiteness of her thighs. I looked away in a sudden pang of sadness. I saw the doll in my mind's eye, and Janet's face. She had come back the next day calm and forgiving, and in all her future visits she never raised directly the issue of my failure with her. I was grateful for her continuing presence, for her forgiveness.

All that is behind me now, I will never come back this way, I tell myself, looking out anxiously for the taxi. It's true, I never really knew any of them anyway, time moved so quickly and I was never in one secure place long enough to form perfect conclusions. In the next three years, allocated my own room in college out of recognition of worth rather than need, I will make lasting friends. Patel's taunt that I want to become a white man is ridiculous. All I want is to escape from this dirt and shame called Balham, this coon condition, this ignorance that prevents me from knowing anything, not even who we are, who they are. How else am I to make sense of what happened to Joseph? The most important thing is to save myself from the misery of his kind of being.

'Oxford can't give you nothing man,' Patel said as I lingered at the doorstep of his shop, unsure of how best to depart, what last desperate words to say to make peace with him. 'It's us lot who have given you everything, and don't you forget that. Oxford has only got money, but the Asian community made you rich.'

I wandered through the streets back to my room, looking hard at everything, trying to understand what were the Balham experiences which Patel claimed were so rich. It was a Saturday afternoon and the pavements were packed with shoppers; I caught snatches of conversations as I passed by, each person seemed to be talking to someone else, but I was not beside any of them long enough to make sense of their speech. The traffic crawled along the main street, the revving of engines or screech of brakes drowning the human voices. In the occasional lull I heard a babble of working-class English, Urdu, Punjabi and the drawl of West Indian accents. Bits of blank paper blew along the pavement, discarded wrappings, or newspapers smudged and screwed up beyond legibility. Headlines in bold print were broken up, making no sense: IMMIGRANTS FLOOD INTO; ROYAL BABY WEIGHS; SEX SCANDAL. Even the grafitti scrawled everywhere was difficult to read, overlapping each other or else written with Eastern lettering.

I passed the cemetery containing Mr Ali's sister and peered through the iron grilles, hoping to catch sight of her tombstone, but there were thousands, a jungle of competing slabs, and my poem was lost among them. Mr Ali knew the spot, he visited every month, but who was Mr Ali to be a reader and critic of my writing?

'You're lucky you're leaving soon,' I told Janet, knowing deep down that I would miss her always. After taking her 'A' levels she was moving to Australia where her father had been awarded an engineering consultancy for three years. She had been excited when she broke the news to me a month ago, bursting into my room, sailing around the table, flopping on the bed and holding out her arms to hug me. Ever since the disaster I had become reluctant to touch her in case she became aroused and I made a fool of myself again. She visited regularly to talk about her literature examination texts with me. I took time off studying the books on my own syllabus to read hers, so that I could discuss them properly with her.

'You are so clever,' she would interrupt, as I held forth on the meaning of this or that passage, startling myself by ideas that flooded into my head from nowhere, by the magic of thinking in words. She would rise from the bed and put her arms around my head, pressing it to her breasts. I recoiled in embarrassment yet at the same time pleased by her appreciation of me. I wanted to hold her, but the memory of previous failure dampened all desire.

'Not really,' I replied nervously, 'it's easy and obvious really, anyone can see what the writer meant.'

'I didn't,' she said, stroking my face, 'so you must be cleverer than most people,' and she planted a kiss loudly and exaggeratedly in my ear, curling her tongue in it so that I squirmed and brightened.

'You have to get a lot of new clothes,' she said, running her hand down my face and neck, alighting on the tear in my collar, 'I can't send you there looking like something from the Congo, stepping off the wall of the World Cruise.' I laughed and pushed her away roughly so that she fell backwards on to the bed, only to bounce back and throw her arms around me. In the several months of regular contact and conversation with me she had lost all shyness in talking about our people to the point of developing a healthy disrespect for our grievances. She would not be impressed or overwhelmed by stories of black distress. I valued her honesty, her refusal to be mawkish and piteous. When Joseph set himself on fire she cried and cried in genuine grief, even though she had only met him once or twice and was in no way responsible for his condition. She soon recovered, pestering me for information about the death, but I could not tell her the truth, mumbling something about a nervous breakdown. I could not tell her that Patel had driven him to it, inadvertently, by dismissing him from his job as camera operator.

Joseph had lost all interest in his work, it appeared. 'He's bloody useless,' Patel complained without looking up from the till where he was busy calculating the contents, 'a total waste of time. I don't know why I took him on in the first place. The whole business is going to rack and ruin because of that stupid nigger.' I mumbled an apology for Joseph, since it was I who had pestered Patel to keep employing him, praising his potential and arguing that all he needed was another chance, a better camera and some more money to live on. Even Shaz who, to begin with, had pitied Joseph and was keen to promote his reputation with Patel, had eventually withdrawn his support, arguing that business was business.

'Nasty, a lot of nastiness they're up to, that Shaz and Patel,' Joseph said, screwing up his face and spitting into a corner of his hovel. He had come back to his hideout and his condition had already deteriorated after only a few days living and sleeping in the dirt. The new clothing which he had bought with his first wages in an attempt to smarten himself up and start life again were soiled. Water leaked from the rafters onto his suitcase, soaking through cracks in the lid and staining the shirts inside.

'What are you going to do now?' I asked, uncomfortable in his presence, wanting to go back to the security of my room and books.

'Fed up with filth. Sex. Sex. Filth,' he said wearily, 'point your camera here. Catch it going in, coming out. Film her mouth when it opening with grief.'

'But it's not the subject, it's the technique that matters, perfecting your knowledge of how the camera works, and how you can make it work for you,' I

234

argued, trying to lift his spirits, reminding him of the original reason why he took employment with Patel. 'At least you got a camera to muck about with.'

He glowered at my unfortunate choice of words and lashed out. 'I don't "muck" with camera. Why you people think that because I got no education I can only fidget with things. The real muck is what Patel doing, all money and sex, dirt and drugs.'

As usual he was right. I had seen the last film he had made that led to his dismissal from Patel's service. It seemed a total failure from the point of view of pornography but in terms of art it had some merit, Joseph obviously trying to distil some clear statement from the mess of bodies. Why else would he have focused on the way the light fell through the window on to the opposite wall, forming bright patches or growing dull according to the passage of clouds. He experimented with all manner of filters and artificial lights, beaming them against the wall, blending them with the sun's rays to create a quiltwork of colours, which he filmed for several minutes. Growing bored, or perhaps by an inexplicable process of inspiration, he interrupted the film by placing the titleboard in front of the camera. He focused on the contours of letters in BOOBY TRAP, the way the B curved in semi-circles like breasts, leading to rounded O's, the shape of lips perhaps, or the space inside an open mouth, before forming breasts again and the Y-like cleavage of thighs. It was as if he was more fascinated by the suggestions made by letters, the subtleties and abstraction of their form, than by the gross actuality before him. Patel was not there to supervise the making of the film, being delayed by a business deal, and Shaz was one of the stars, so Joseph could do what he liked with the camera. No one noticed where he pointed it. The eight bodies, also left to their own devices, were too knotted in a ball of lust to bother with him. Now and again the film showed pieces of naked bodies as someone pressed another momentarily against the wall or jerked into the field of vision. The camera ran on for forty minutes or so, when Joseph suddenly switched it off and left, the orgy continuing until Patel returned.

'Is the skeleton what matter, not the flesh,' he argued when Patel spluttered with rage, 'the spaces between one rib and the next.' He had booked the eight boys and girls for four hours, guaranteeing fifteen pounds an hour for their services. A week's profit in the shop had been invested in the half-day's filming, and all of it had been wasted. In addition he had given Joseph a sub of fifty pounds as encouragement. The trial runs, whilst not wholly satisfactory in terms of film techniques, were good enough to suggest that Joseph was learning fast enough to risk the making of BOOBY TRAP. Patel had accordingly laid out money on his stars, bought extra lights and equipment and furnished the room with expensive accoutrements: pink cushions, velvety sheets, a deep sofa, Turkish-looking carpets to give an exotic feel, and a four-poster bed with an assortment of leather thongs, uniforms and frilly underclothing hanging from the railing around it.

'The words is the space in the skeleton,' he tried desperately to explain, 'everything else sweaty, one big wet mess, but the skeleton pure and white and dry, more real, is the skeleton what's gonna last throughout time.'

Patel dismissed him on the spot, chasing him from his premises.

'So where are you heading now?' I asked, as he fumbled in the suitcase, found a soggy apple and bit into it.

He chewed slowly, saying nothing, deliberating on the question, 'Anywhere,' he said after a while, 'prison. The same really.'

'Why don't you head north and find your father?' I suggested, trying to be helpful, 'and start all over again.'

'Sure,' he replied, 'but tell me where he lost first so I'll find him.'

I left his hideout and headed for Patel's shop, hoping to persuade him to exercise charity. At least he could give him the fares for the trip north. Perhaps it was not a good idea, perhaps his father was like mine, utterly careless in the way he created children and equally unconcerned in abandoning them. It had been over six years since I last saw him. Out of guilt, or perhaps to claim various benefits from the Social Security, he had written my mother asking her to send me over. He changed his mind soon after, but by that time I was already in England, sharing a dingy council flat with him for several months, until he handed me over to the Welfare people. I rarely saw him, perhaps once a week when he gave me money to buy food from the take-away shops on the High Street. He was always drunk when he came home, and would grunt a greeting then fall asleep. By the time I awoke in the morning, he was gone.

She was surprised to get his letter. It had been two years since he had disappeared, taking all the money in the bank and cashing in his life policy. When he left, without so much as a note, I was relieved that none of the village boys were around to compose a mocking calypso. I felt sorry for the way we had treated Peter. My mother was glad to get rid of me, one less mouth to feed. She was thinking too of my future in a country teeming with schools and universities. There was nothing to do in Guyana, what with how the black people running things, she calculated, soon the place would be one big pit and latrine, but in England I would grow up properly, take education, get prestige job, make good marriage, and send money back home to help them out. She planned that eventually I would send for all of them. Coolie people had no future in Guyana, she was convinced. And the black people were so tribal. They rather starve (and they soon would, mark my words, she said) than let better, more knowing and skilful Indian people rule with them. Slavery dirty up their minds and it was too late for them to recover. They either be boss or they be slave – they don't know how to compromise like Indian.

'Ma, is true all black people ignorant?' I asked, thinking of Caesar, a black boy in my class who sold mangoes every Saturday at the market, beside Auntie Pakul's stall. No matter how hard Miss Lambert our teacher tried with him, he still couldn't do sums.

'You are an utter dunce,' Miss Lambert told him, smacking him on the head. We all laughed at him. Miss Lambert was black but she knew how to multiply.

My grandmother looked sternly at me and told me to hush my mouth. 'Why you be so ungrateful,' she scolded me, 'and Clarice feeding you with guava from she tree and mauby from she pot. One day you go grow up and say I ignorant, not so?'

I looked sheepishly at my feet.

'Go and wash you tongue out,' she ordered, and I went with meek expression on my face to the tub, dipped a calabash full of water, swilled it and spat it out. I watched her from afar peeling a pumpkin for tonight's supper knowing that she was a stupid old woman, more stupid than Caesar. I fooled Caesar, and if she thinks I'm sorry, then she's a bigger fool. Caesar was sitting on the bare concrete floor of the market, his family too poor to afford a raised stall, a rice-bag spread before him, on which he had arranged his dozen mangoes. I prodded them, feeling for the softest and ripest.

'How much you want for this mango?' I asked in a loud voice. I knew he was afraid of me, because I was no dunce, I was Miss Lambert's favourite.

'Twenty cents,' he said shyly.

I stood before his mangoes, put on a look of disgust and spat on the ground. 'Twenty cents for this rotten mango! What daylight robbery you doing?'

'Ten cents then,' he mumbled quickly. He was so timid that he would have given me the mango free, to get rid of me.

'What you say? Five cents?' looking down at him.

'Yes,' he said. He avoided my eyes, stretching forth his hand like a beggar to take my twenty-five cent coin.

'Make sure you give me right change, I know how you does cheat people.'

He turned over a few coins from his pocket, calculating my change.

'How much is five from twenty-five?' I asked him, assuming a serious tone of voice like Miss Lambert. He looked all confused. He shoved out his hand full of coins for me to take my own change. 'Five from twenty-five is twenty-two,' I said, picking out two ten-cent coins and a penny. He smiled with relief, and put the rest of the money back into his pocket, thanking me for my help.

'I'm not giving that nigger another penny,' Patel swore. 'Why should I? I don't know why you're so sorry for him.'

I said nothing. It would be difficult to explain to him that I was trying to make up after all these years for cheating Caesar.

'Because he deserves it, and he needs help, that's why,' I replied in a pleading voice, 'and there's no need to call him a nigger. He's one of us and we're one of him.'

Patel was adamant, however. 'Look!' he said, pointing his finger in my face, 'you gotta get hard in this life. All those books have made your head soft and rotten, always sorry for people. "He needs help" my arse! The only need I supply I do for hard cash. I'm no social welfare officer. If they need sex, I give them films, if they need to get high I supply. Here – ' he reached under the counter and fished out a small plastic packet of white powder, 'you know what this is?'

I looked at it ignorantly.

'That's more precious than a boat-load of ivory, man. Ten pounds' worth of cocaine you're holding in your hand, all the way from Sri Lanka. I can sell fifty thousand packets a year, but I can't get enough of the stuff. You know how much cash that is? White people will pay and pay and pay, they'd eat their mothers and bugger their grandmothers just to get hold of this powder, just to put it up their nose. I tell you, they're more crazy than coons! I give some of the girls a packet each, and they take off their clothes and screw anybody, man, boy, animal or each other in front of the camera, all day if needs be, just for that. You should see them scrambling at my hand for the powder, they beg, they strip, you should see them eating each other naked.' He reached under the counter, located a sex cassette, and gave it to me. 'Take this to Oxford and show it to all the white boys. You'll be popular overnight with them. Here, take this packet too and sell it for twice what I sell it for, they can afford it, what with all their wealthy daddies. No need to worry about college fees and rent. I'll supply you with the powder, and you can set up shop there. I'll give you ten per cent commission – you'll end up rich for once in your life.'

*   *   *

'I'm glad you're going away to Australia,' I confessed on the bus as she took me to Oxford Street, the day before I left for university. She expected me to be depressed, and was startled by my statement. 'It's a new beginning for you, a new, clean country. England is so messy and violent and drugged up, everything is going to pot.'

She laughed at the unintended pun. 'You sound like an old wise man already and you've not even started at university!'

I knew though that I was right, for I had already betrayed her with Monica. I was as shop-soiled as all the things Patel dealt in.

'No, but you're pure, you know,' I said in a hesitant voice, unsure of what I really wanted to express.

'You mean I'm still a virgin?' she replied mischievously.

I felt wounded by her accusation and kept quiet until we reached the shops, trying to work out in my mind what it was I felt about her this past year.

'Dirt is not as dirty as you think,' she interrupted, 'that's why some men go with whores. They need it. They can't do it with clean women.' She looked into my eyes with such fierce honesty that I had to turn away. It was as if she had known all along, by some mystery of intuition, that I had slept with Monica.

'You mean to say it's alright for men to go off with whores?'

'No, it's not alright, but if they do, they shouldn't be such hypocrites, and start mouthing off or mourning about purity. It's all that daffodils stuff again, all that mental sniffing at petals for fragrance.'

'But you are fragrant, you are everything I intended,' I blurted out, the words seeming to come from nowhere, and as soon as they were uttered, sounding foolish. In one accidental sentence I had finally confessed all the dreams that I had stuttered out to her in a year of meetings, always trying to structure the expression of my desire for her so as to make it impersonal, philosophic, universal, but always failing, my plain needs leaking through the cracks in words. Although embarrassed, I was still relieved that it was said, that it was all over. 'Of course the road to hell is paved with all those cobblestones,' I continued, in as casual a voice as possible, and shrugging my shoulders, to cover up my weakness. I suddenly felt old and tired and done for. I wanted the bus to stop. I wanted to get off. All the stopping and starting was making me sick. I wanted to stop moving. I didn't want to go anywhere anymore. I didn't want to be born time and again. I didn't want to be an eternal, indefinite immigrant. I wanted to get off.

She bought me a white shirt when we reached the shops. She made me try it on in a booth and inspected me when I emerged, pulling at the sleeves, looking at the shoulders. I turned around so that she could be sure. She turned me round again and again, screwing up her eyes and peering intently. I felt like one of Shaz's whores, or a slave on an auction block.

'It suits you perfectly,' she said, with the authority of a mother.

As I stripped off in the booth I noticed my body in the mirror. It looked meagre and unworthy of attention.

I was glad there was no one to see me in my nakedness through some slot.

'It fits your body well,' she said, 'it goes nicely against your brown skin. I love the colour of your skin,' running her fingers on the back of my hand. 'And make sure you wash it properly and keep it white, and don't spill ink on it. It's not for writing on. All that silly poetry you come out with you can keep on the page.'

I am wearing her clean white shirt as I wait for my taxi. I have promised her that when she returns from Australia I will wear the same spotless shirt on my first visit to her home as a sign of my faithfulness to her. I am to be like a medieval knight bearing about his body some secret token of his lady. It would be our private, sentimental game. Up to now our whole relationship has been private. I have guarded her from Shaz's questioning, refusing to report on the progress of our relationship, and she has guarded me from her parents, who would in all probability ban her from writing to me.

'I can't really tell my parents,' she confessed early on, 'they wouldn't understand.'

'It's alright,' I said, hurt by her admission, 'it doesn't matter, does it?'

'I'd like you to come home though, to see my room, all my things . . .'

'It's fine just seeing them in photographs,' I replied. The truth though was that whilst I couldn't imagine being in her home, I still longed for the calmness of it, the sense of place, the sense of belonging. Living in rented rooms and public spaces, I had never known any intimacy with everyday furniture, and the security and pleasure to be got from being surrounded by owned things, your own things. It must be so satisfying to have your name on your bedroom door, and a pretty plaque wreathed with flowers, 'Janet's Room', knowing that the sign was defining you against intruders, revealing your only-ness. I wished Mr Ali had allowed my name at the end of the verse I wrote for his sister's tombstone. It was in the open, exposed to all weathers, and in a clutter of other tombstones, all similarly shaped and indistinguishable from each other, but still it was in stone, chiselled in stone, you could run your finger in the grooves of letters, knowing that they were your own, that they would take a lifetime to wear away.

As she gave me the white shirt, and kissed me on the cheek saying goodbye, she promised that in three years' time, when we met up, she would introduce me to her parents. I will be my own photograph then, sharply defined, not like the unrecognisable blurs in Joseph's incompetent films. I will have become somebody definite, my education compensating for my colour in the eyes of her parents. In the meantime we will exist only for each other. I will be her dark secret, her illicit pregnancy, her undeveloped child. We laughed uneasily. Although I had long reassured her that I forgave the prejudice of her parents, I couldn't help finding consolation in Patel's feelings for white people. 'All they have over us is money,' Patel said, getting worked up when I argued the merits of my books against his films, 'and any monkey can make money, once you learn the trick. Soon we'll have more than them, and England will be one tribe of Patels. English people will have names like Lucinda Patel and Egbert Smythe-Patel, wait and see boy.' When I ridiculed his bigotry, he grew even more incensed, cursing me in a personal way. 'Just because you ain't got a mother don't mean that England will mother you, you stupid mother-fucker. All you're looking for is somebody to mother you. Why don't you grow up and be yourself instead of mourning for white pussy?'

Three years, she said, but that amount of time is meaningless, I cannot conceive of it. The future is a space only in daydreams, as soon as I blink it shrinks to a dot the size of my pupils. I only know *now*, and what used to be. I watch the clouds being rinsed to their original colour and the darkness slowly unpeeling from the sky. I wait under the streetlamp, wanting to be visible, but the light flames upon my head, flames upon my skin and I have to step back into the shade. Soon the black cab will come scuttling along the road like a beetle. Its bright eyes will pick me up like prey, and soon I'll be gone, me and all my things. One last breath, then I'll climb in and be gone.

Also available in Minerva

AMIT CHAUDHURI

A Strange and Sublime Address

'Shot through with poetry. A small jewel of a work, perfectly cut and polished'
Francis King

'Sandeep, who lives with his parents in a Bombay high-rise, plunges eagerly into the life of his uncle's extended family in Calcutta; everything he sees and hears . . . is touched with magic'
Independent on Sunday

'Funny, delicate, sensuous, evocative . . . made me laugh aloud. The best portrait of India today I've read'
Margaret Drabble

'A boy's world is conjured with total credibility, a way of life looked at with some sharpness, some tenderness, some irony . . . a perfect, small achievement'
Isabel Quigly, *Financial Times*

'Numerous daily events – unremarkable in themselves – assume a bloated yet magnificent significance under Chaudhuri's tutelage'
Simon Cunliffe, *Independent*

'This evocation of the routine, quotidian magic of normality strikes me as an extraordinary thing to have brought off . . . mesmerising'
John Lanchester, *Vogue*

'Raptly luminous . . . there is no ordinary writer here'
Christopher Wordsworth, *Guardian*

GLORIA NAYLOR

Linden Hills

Linden Hills is a rich, private residential estate in America. Intended as a symbol that blacks can be just like white, Linden Hills is in fact an infernal place, and as two young blacks, Willie and Lester, odd-job their way down the hill in the week before Christmas, the layers of hypocrisy and self-destruction which are its foundation become exposed.

And at the bottom of the hill waits the estate's sinister owner, Luther Nedeed, feudal baron of the estate and of his own family, whose perpetuation of the cruel, inverted values of Linden Hills must ultimately be confronted.

'Next to Toni Morrison, . . . she creates the most complex black women characters in modern literature'
Women's Review of Books

'A clever, subtle book'
London Review of Books

'The characters, atmosphere and dialogue (are) compelling . . . will no doubt strengthen her reputation as one of the most important new novelists in the United States'
Books and Bookmen

A Selected List of Fiction Available from Minerva

While every effort is made to keep prices low, it is sometimes necessary to increase prices at short notice. Mandarin Paperbacks reserves the right to show new retail prices on covers which may differ from those previously advertised in the text or elsewhere.

The prices shown below were correct at the time of going to press.

☐	7493 9145 6	**Love and Death on Long Island**	Gilbert Adair	£4.99
☐	7493 9130 8	**The War of Don Emmanuel's Nether Parts**	Louis de Bernieres	£5.99
☐	7493 9903 1	**Dirty Faxes**	Andrew Davies	£4.99
☐	7493 9056 5	**Nothing Natural**	Jenny Diski	£4.99
☐	7493 9173 1	**The Trick is to Keep Breathing**	Janice Galloway	£4.99
☐	7493 9124 3	**Honour Thy Father**	Lesley Glaister	£4.99
☐	7493 9918 X	**Richard's Feet**	Carey Harrison	£6.99
☐	7493 9028 X	**Not Not While the Giro**	James Kelman	£4.99
☐	7493 9112 X	**Hopeful Monsters**	Nicholas Mosley	£6.99
☐	7493 9029 8	**Head to Toe**	Joe Orton	£4.99
☐	7493 9117 0	**The Good Republic**	William Palmer	£5.99
☐	7493 9162 6	**Four Bare Legs in a Bed**	Helen Simpson	£4.99
☐	7493 9134 0	**Rebuilding Coventry**	Sue Townsend	£4.99
☐	7493 9151 0	**Boating for Beginners**	Jeanette Winterson	£4.99
☐	7493 9915 5	**Cyrus Cyrus**	Adam Zameenzad	£7.99

All these books are available at your bookshop or newsagent, or can be ordered direct from the publisher. Just tick the titles you want and fill in the form below.

Mandarin Paperbacks, Cash Sales Department, PO Box 11, Falmouth, Cornwall TR10 9EN.

Please send cheque or postal order, no currency, for purchase price quoted and allow the following for postage and packing:

UK including BFPO   £1.00 for the first book, 50p for the second and 30p for each additional book ordered to a maximum charge of £3.00.

Overseas including Eire   £2 for the first book, £1.00 for the second and 50p for each additional book thereafter.

NAME (Block letters) ....

ADDRESS..

....

☐ I enclose my remittance for ....

☐ I wish to pay by Access/Visa Card Number ☐☐☐☐☐☐☐☐☐☐☐☐☐☐☐☐

Expiry Date ☐☐☐☐